MORE PRAISE FOR BABYMOUSE!

"Sassy, smart . . . Babymouse is here to stay."
—The Horn Book Magazine

"Young readers will happily fall in line."
—Kirkus Reviews

"The brother-sister creative team hits the mark with humor, sweetness, and characters so genuine they can pass for real kids." —Booklist

"Babymouse is spunky, ambitious, and, at times, a total dweeb."
—School Library Journal

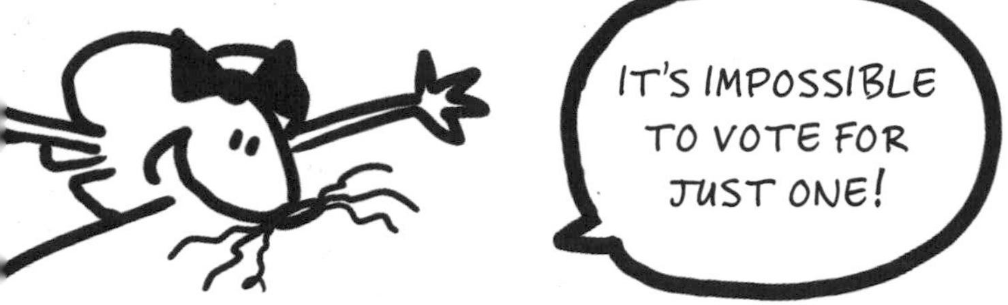
IT'S IMPOSSIBLE TO VOTE FOR JUST ONE!

BE SURE TO READ **ALL** THE **BABYMOUSE** BOOKS:

#1 BABYMOUSE: Queen of the World!
#2 BABYMOUSE: Our Hero
#3 BABYMOUSE: Beach Babe
#4 BABYMOUSE: Rock Star
#5 BABYMOUSE: Heartbreaker
#6 CAMP BABYMOUSE
#7 BABYMOUSE: Skater Girl
#8 BABYMOUSE: Puppy Love
#9 BABYMOUSE: Monster Mash
#10 BABYMOUSE: The Musical
#11 BABYMOUSE: Dragonslayer
#12 BABYMOUSE: Burns Rubber
#13 BABYMOUSE: Cupcake Tycoon
#14 BABYMOUSE: Mad Scientist
#15 A Very BABYMOUSE Christmas
#16 BABYMOUSE for President

FOR PRESIDENT

SEAL OF THE PRESIDENT OF THE UNITED STATES OF CUPCAKES

BY JENNIFER L. HOLM & MATTHEW HOLM

RANDOM HOUSE NEW YORK

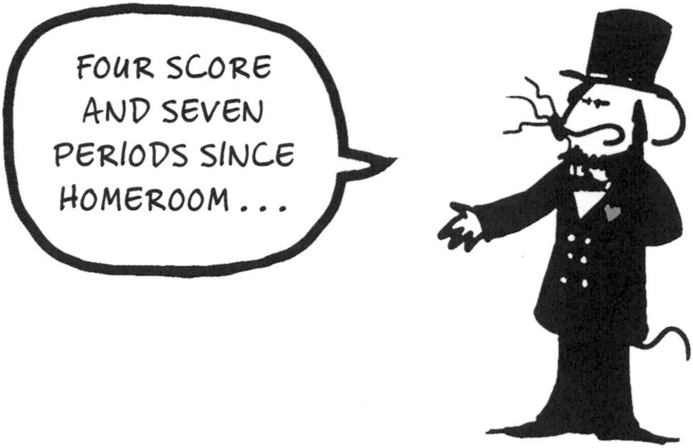
FOUR SCORE AND SEVEN PERIODS SINCE HOMEROOM . . .

Published in the United States by Random House Children's Books, a division of Random House, Inc., New York.

Random House and the colophon are registered trademarks of Random House, Inc.

Visit us on the Web! randomhouse.com/kids

Educators and librarians, for a variety of teaching tools, visit us at randomhouse.com/teachers

Babymouse.com

Library of Congress Cataloging-in-Publication Data
Babymouse for president / by Jennifer L. Holm and Matthew Holm. — 1st ed.
p. cm.
Summary: When Babymouse decides to become president of the student council, she learns that there is more to running for office than being famous and in charge.
ISBN 978-0-375-86780-4 (trade pbk.) — ISBN 978-0-375-96780-1 (lib. bdg.)
1. Graphic novels. [1. Graphic novels. 2. Politics, Practical—Fiction. 3. Schools—Fiction. 4. Mice—Fiction.] I. Holm, Matthew. II. Title.
PZ7.7.H65Baff 2012 741.5'973—dc23 2011024118

MANUFACTURED IN MALAYSIA
10 9 8 7 6 5 4 3 2 1
First Edition

Random House Children's Books supports the First Amendment and celebrates the right to read.

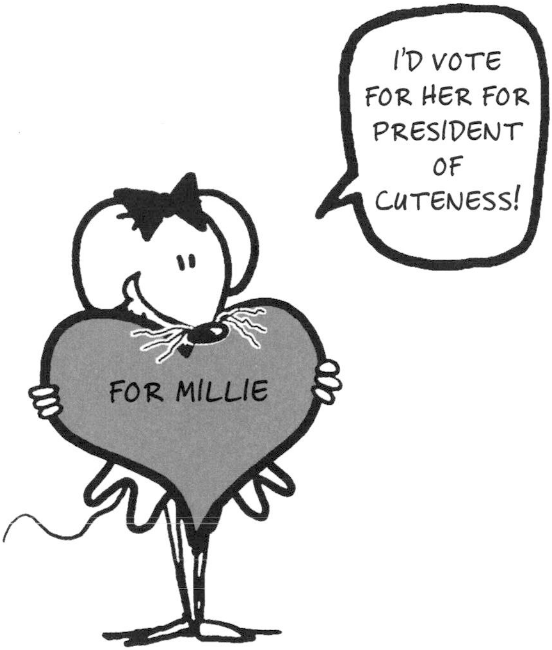
I'D VOTE FOR HER FOR PRESIDENT OF CUTENESS!
FOR MILLIE

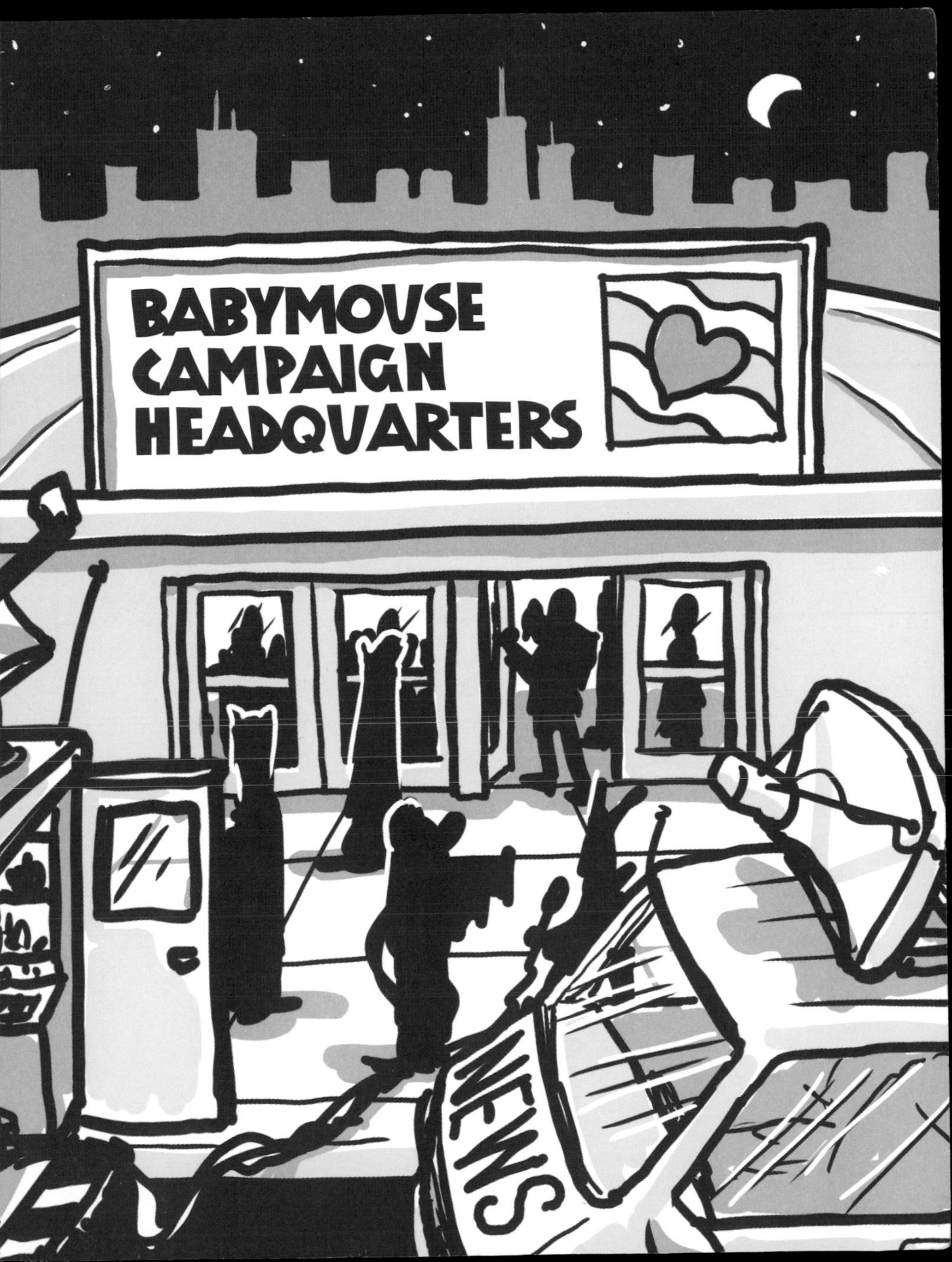
BABYMOUSE
CAMPAIGN
HEADQUARTERS
NEWS

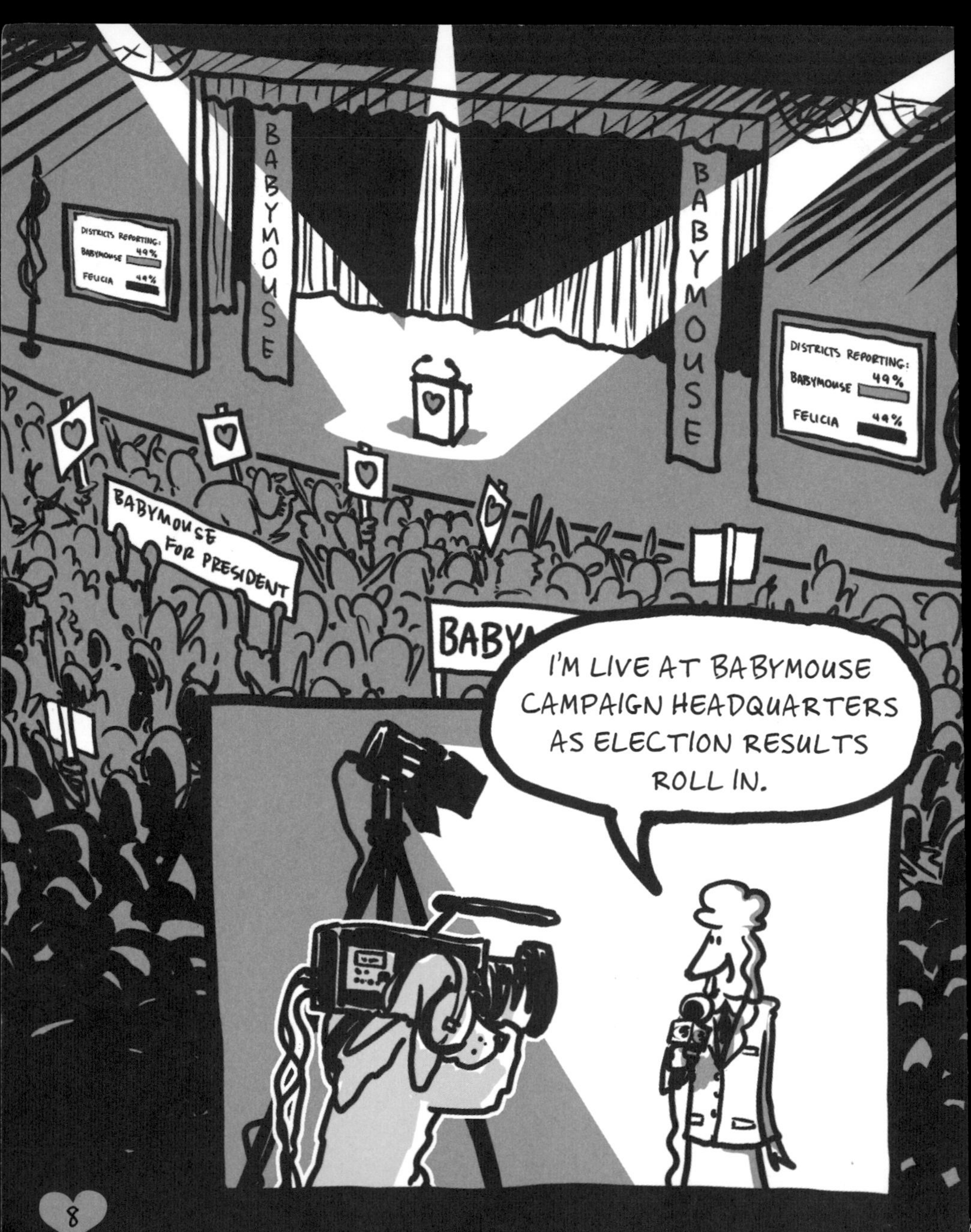
BABYMOUSE
BABYMOUSE
DISTRICTS REPORTING:
BABYMOUSE 49%
FELICIA 49%
DISTRICTS REPORTING:
BABYMOUSE 49%
FELICIA 49%
BABYMOUSE FOR PRESIDENT
I'M LIVE AT BABYMOUSE CAMPAIGN HEADQUARTERS AS ELECTION RESULTS ROLL IN.

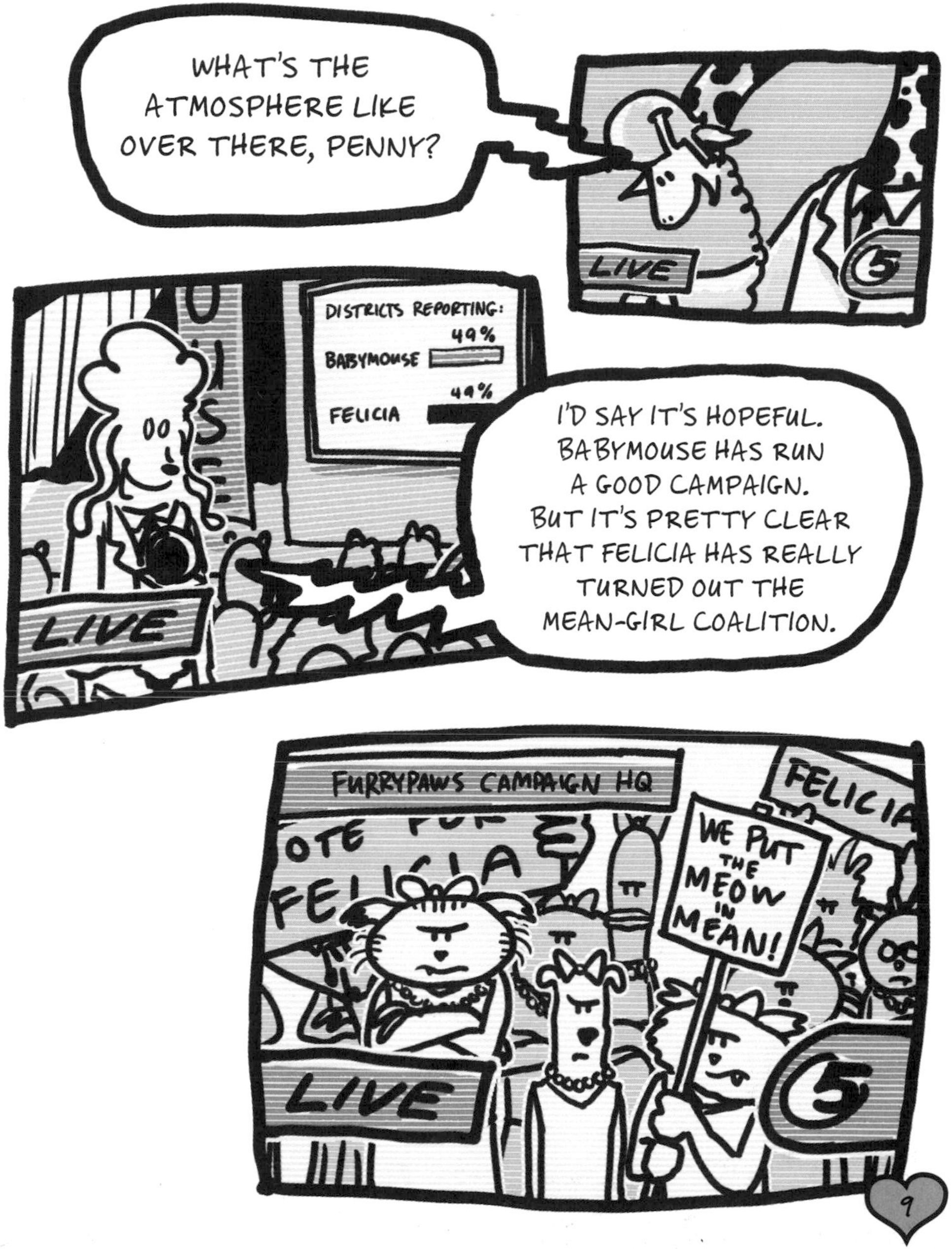
WHAT'S THE ATMOSPHERE LIKE OVER THERE, PENNY?
LIVE
5
DISTRICTS REPORTING:
49%
BABYMOUSE
49%
FELICIA
LIVE
I'D SAY IT'S HOPEFUL. BABYMOUSE HAS RUN A GOOD CAMPAIGN. BUT IT'S PRETTY CLEAR THAT FELICIA HAS REALLY TURNED OUT THE MEAN-GIRL COALITION.
FURRYPAWS CAMPAIGN HQ
FELICIA
WE PUT THE MEOW IN MEAN!
LIVE
5

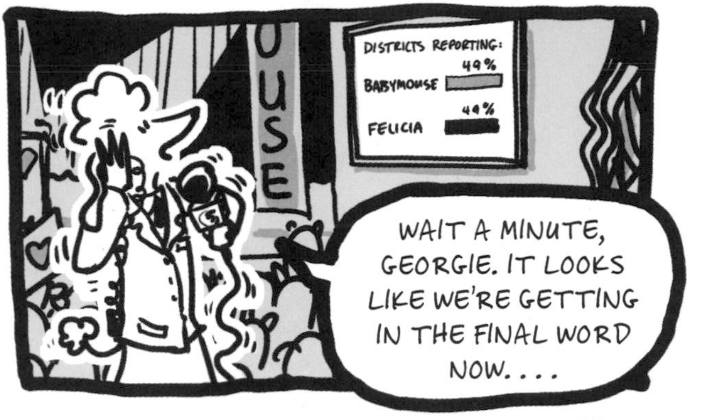
DISTRICTS REPORTING:
49%
BABYMOUSE
49%
FELICIA
OUSE
WAIT A MINUTE, GEORGIE. IT LOOKS LIKE WE'RE GETTING IN THE FINAL WORD NOW. . . .

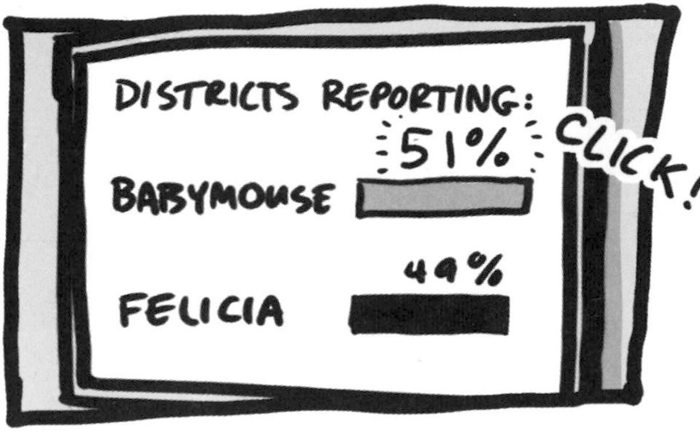
DISTRICTS REPORTING:
51%
BABYMOUSE
49%
FELICIA
CLICK!

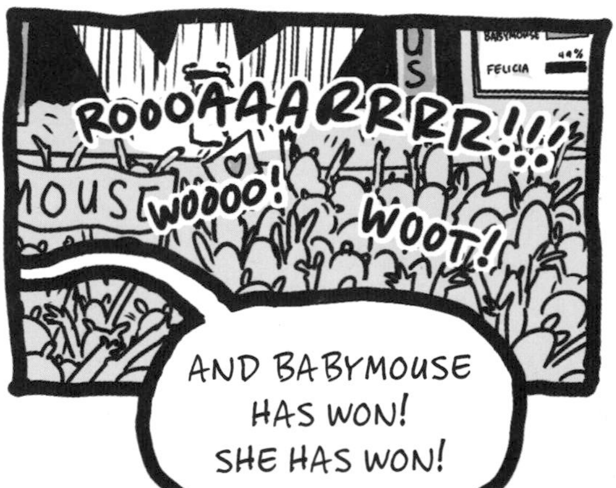
FELICIA
49%
ROOOAAAARRRR!!!
MOUS
WOOOO!
WOOT!
AND BABYMOUSE HAS WON! SHE HAS WON!

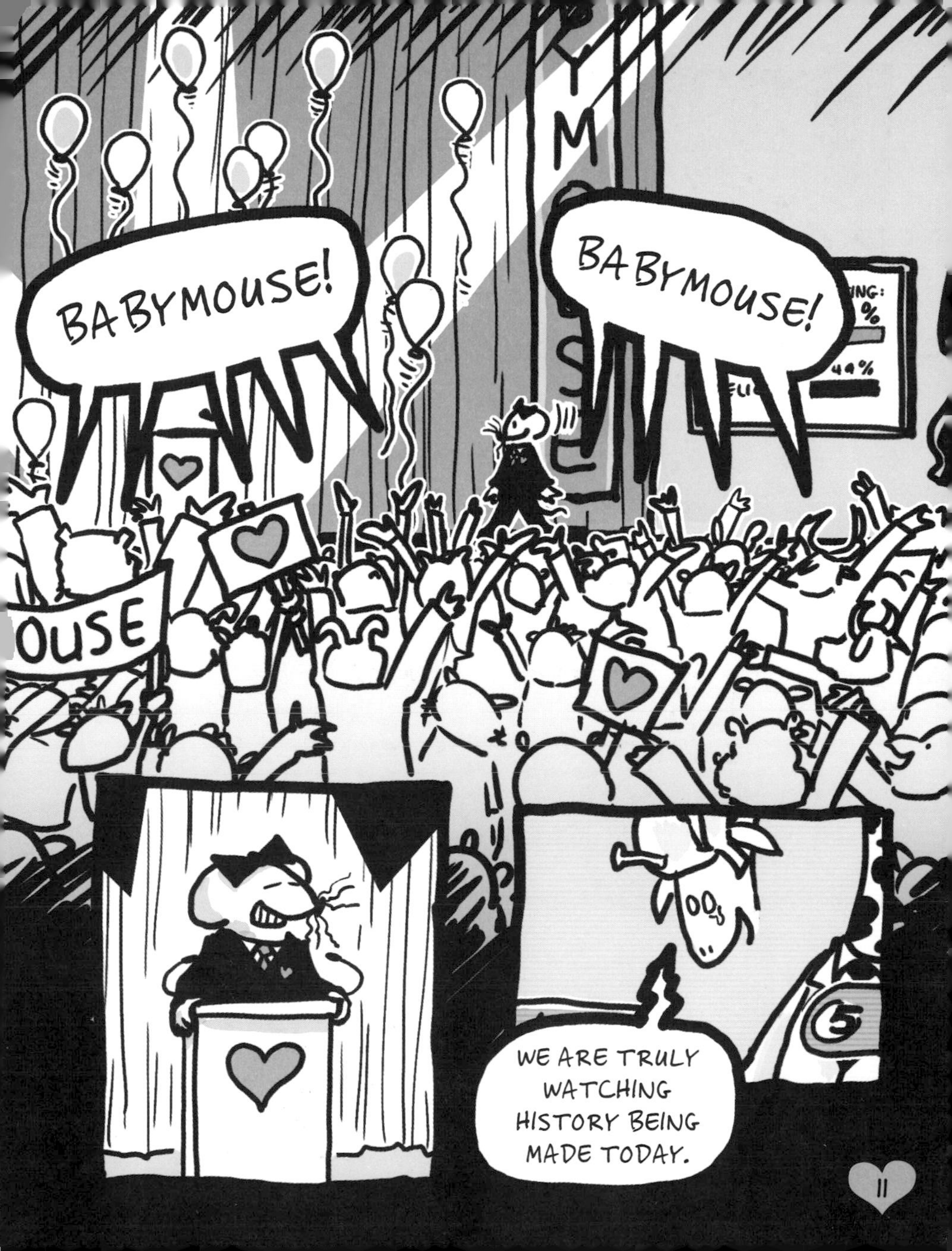
BABYMOUSE!
BABYMOUSE!
WE ARE TRULY WATCHING HISTORY BEING MADE TODAY.

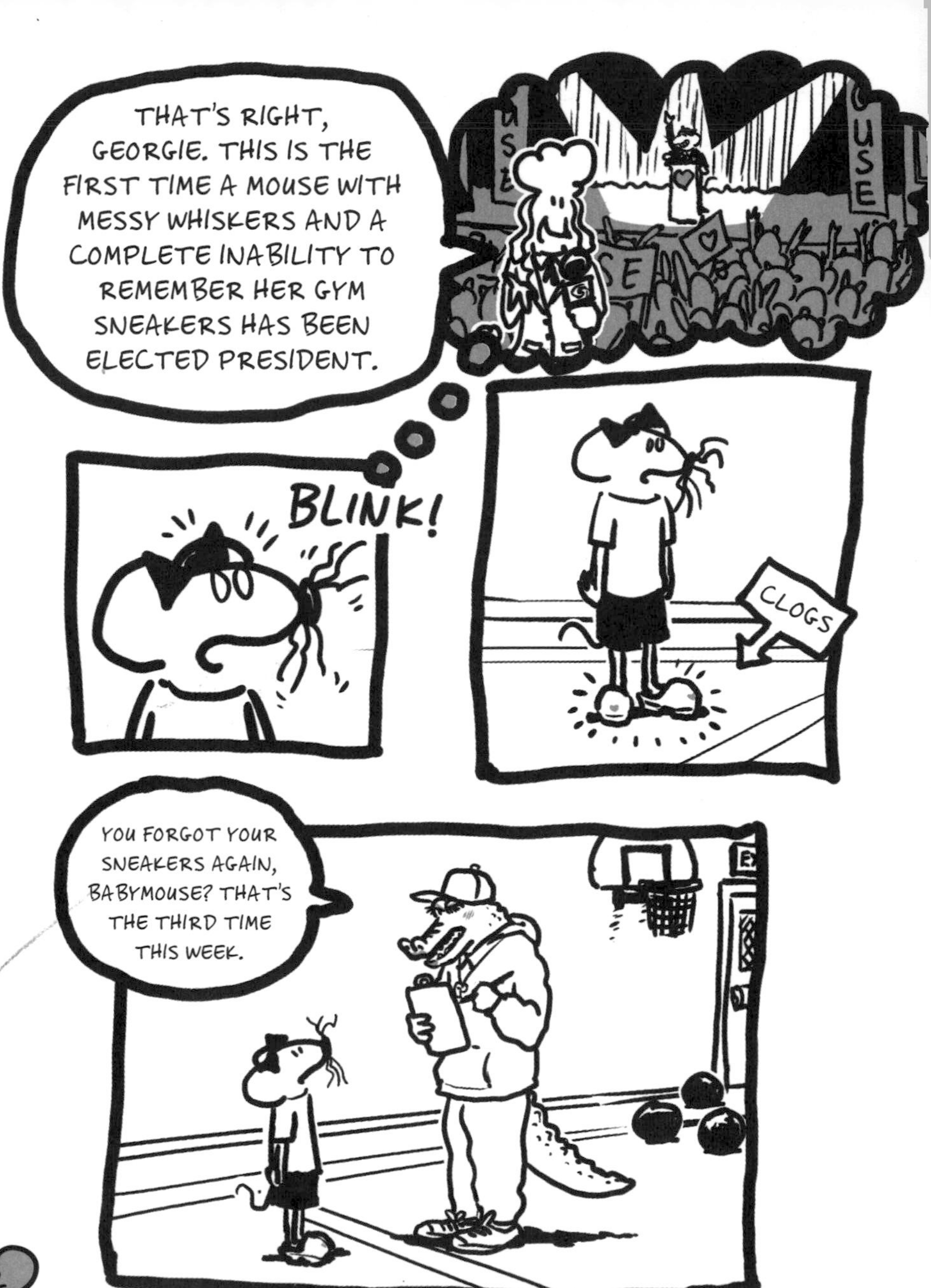

THAT'S RIGHT, GEORGIE. THIS IS THE FIRST TIME A MOUSE WITH MESSY WHISKERS AND A COMPLETE INABILITY TO REMEMBER HER GYM SNEAKERS HAS BEEN ELECTED PRESIDENT.
BLINK!
CLOGS
YOU FORGOT YOUR SNEAKERS AGAIN, BABYMOUSE? THAT'S THE THIRD TIME THIS WEEK.

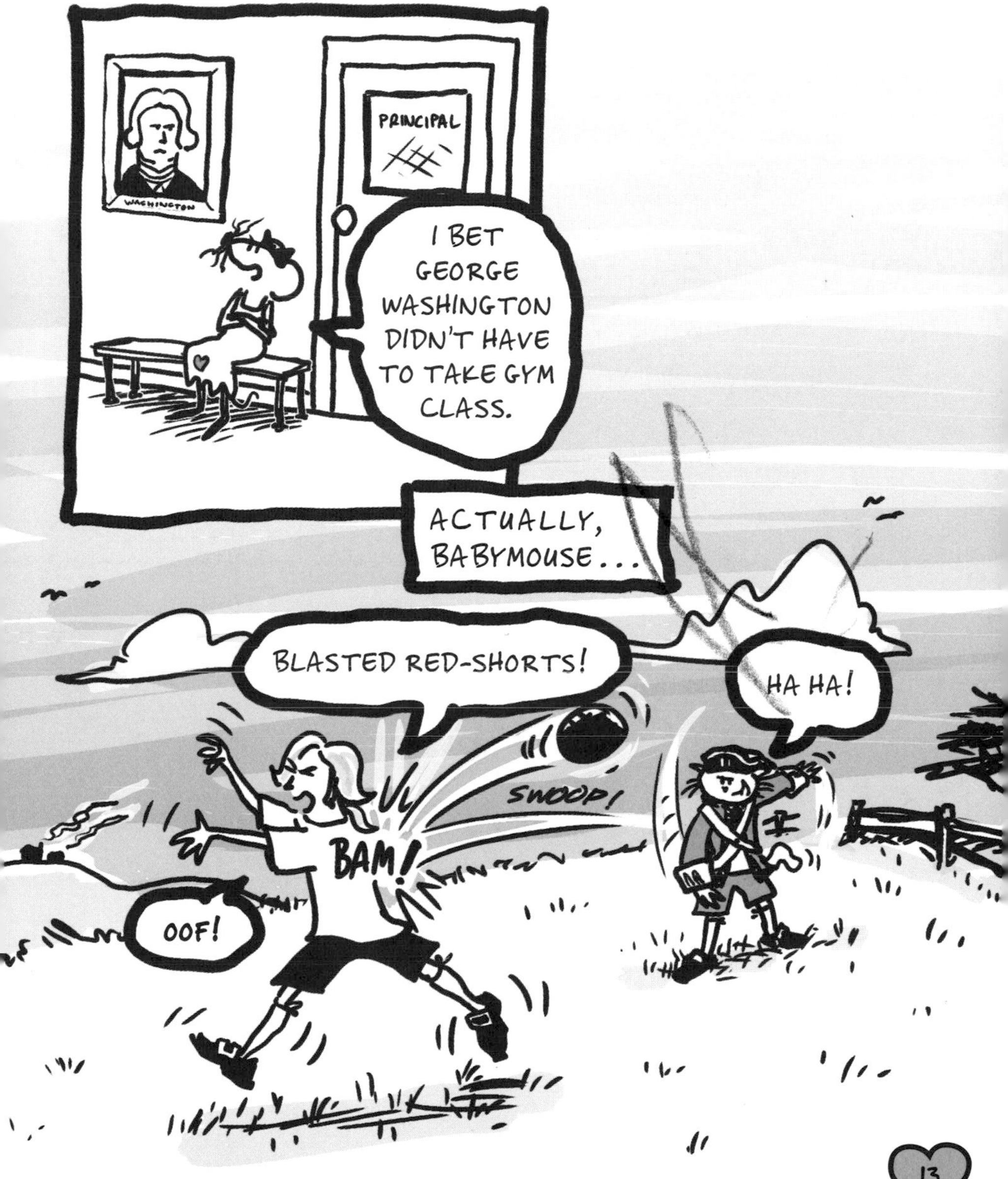
PRINCIPAL
WASHINGTON
I BET GEORGE WASHINGTON DIDN'T HAVE TO TAKE GYM CLASS.
ACTUALLY, BABYMOUSE...
BLASTED RED-SHORTS!
HA HA!
SWOOP!
BAM!
OOF!

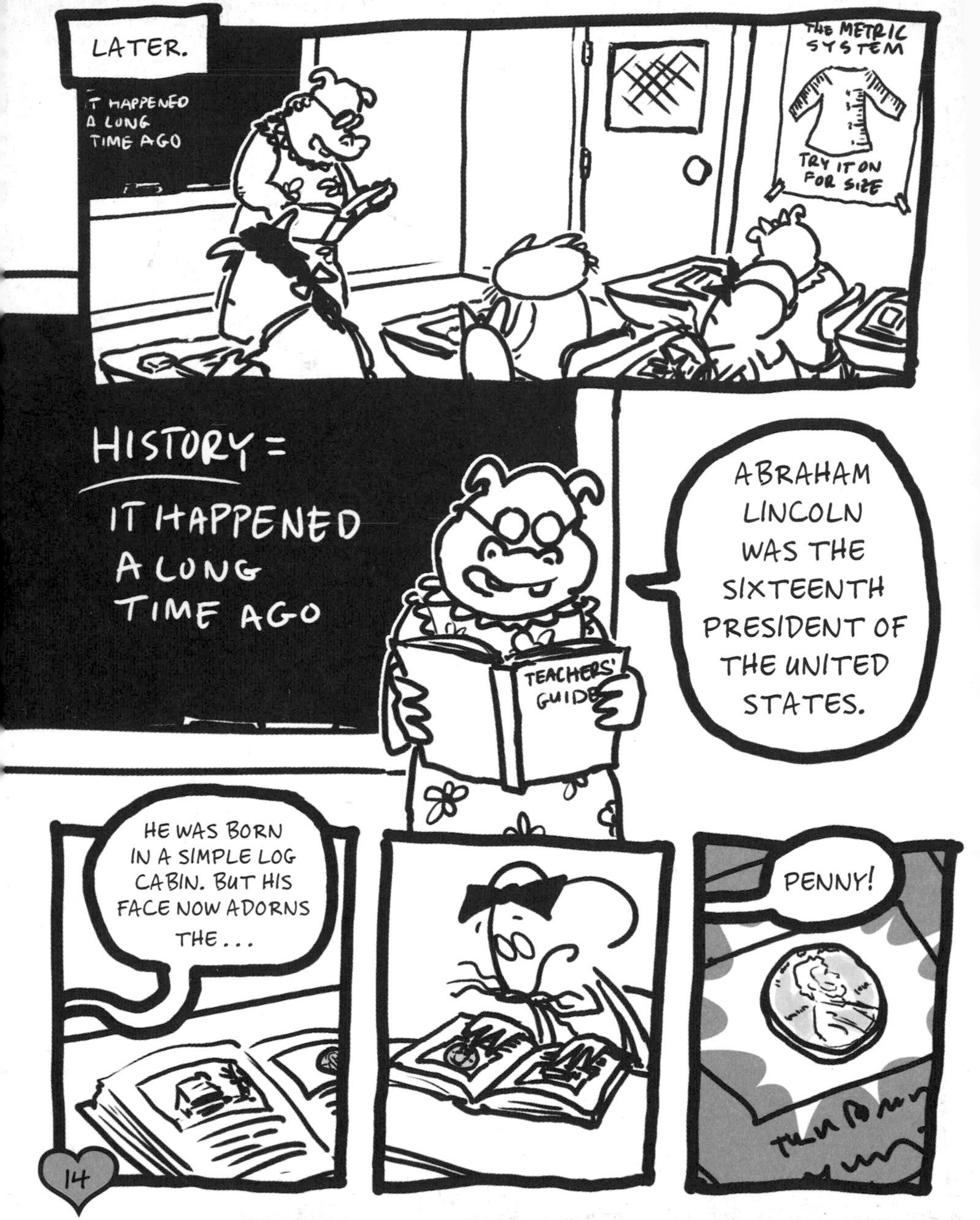
LATER.
IT HAPPENED A LONG TIME AGO
THE METRIC SYSTEM
TRY IT ON FOR SIZE
HISTORY =
IT HAPPENED A LONG TIME AGO
ABRAHAM LINCOLN WAS THE SIXTEENTH PRESIDENT OF THE UNITED STATES.
TEACHERS' GUIDE
HE WAS BORN IN A SIMPLE LOG CABIN. BUT HIS FACE NOW ADORNS THE . . .
PENNY!

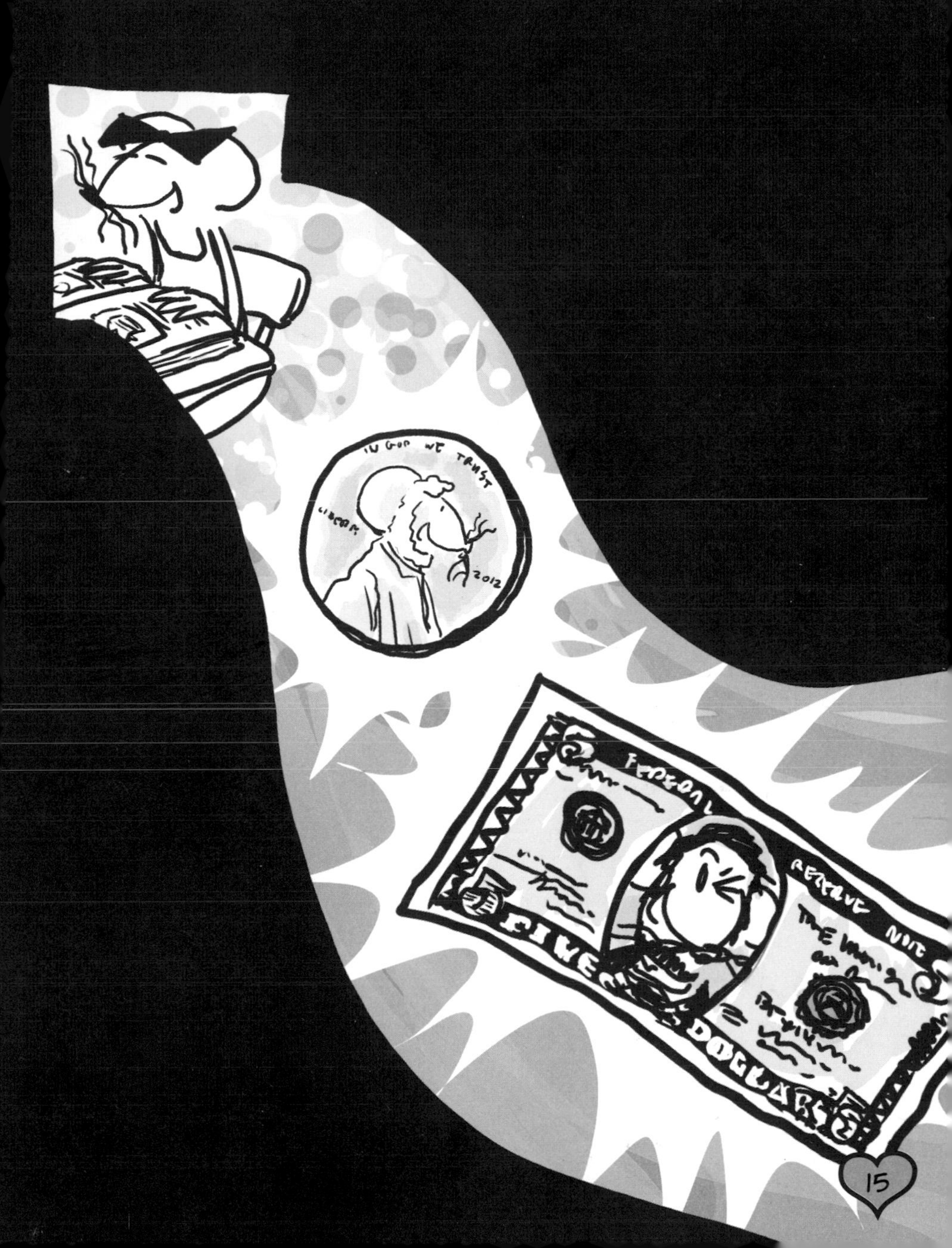
IN GOD WE TRUST
2012
FIVE
DOLLARS

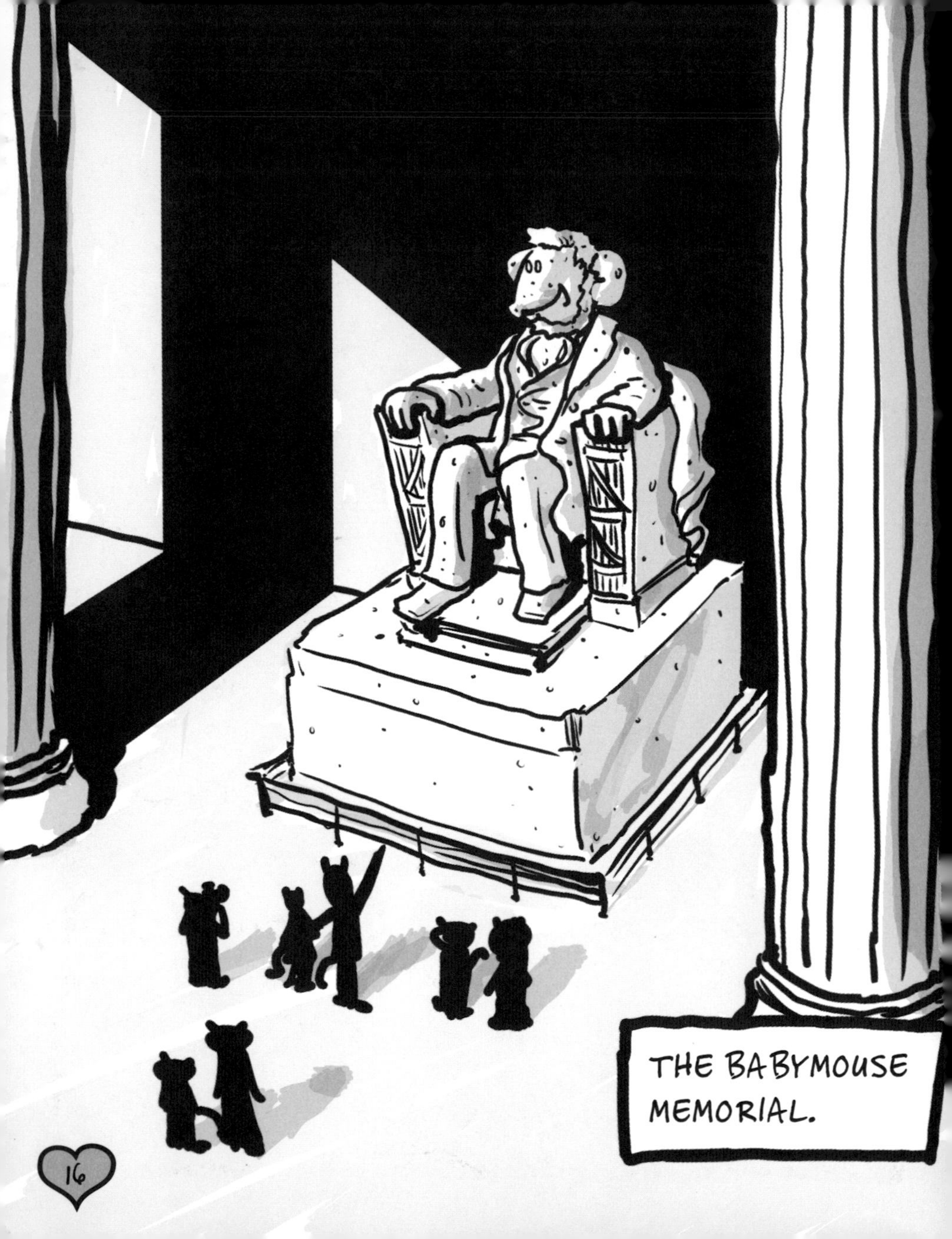
THE BABYMOUSE MEMORIAL.

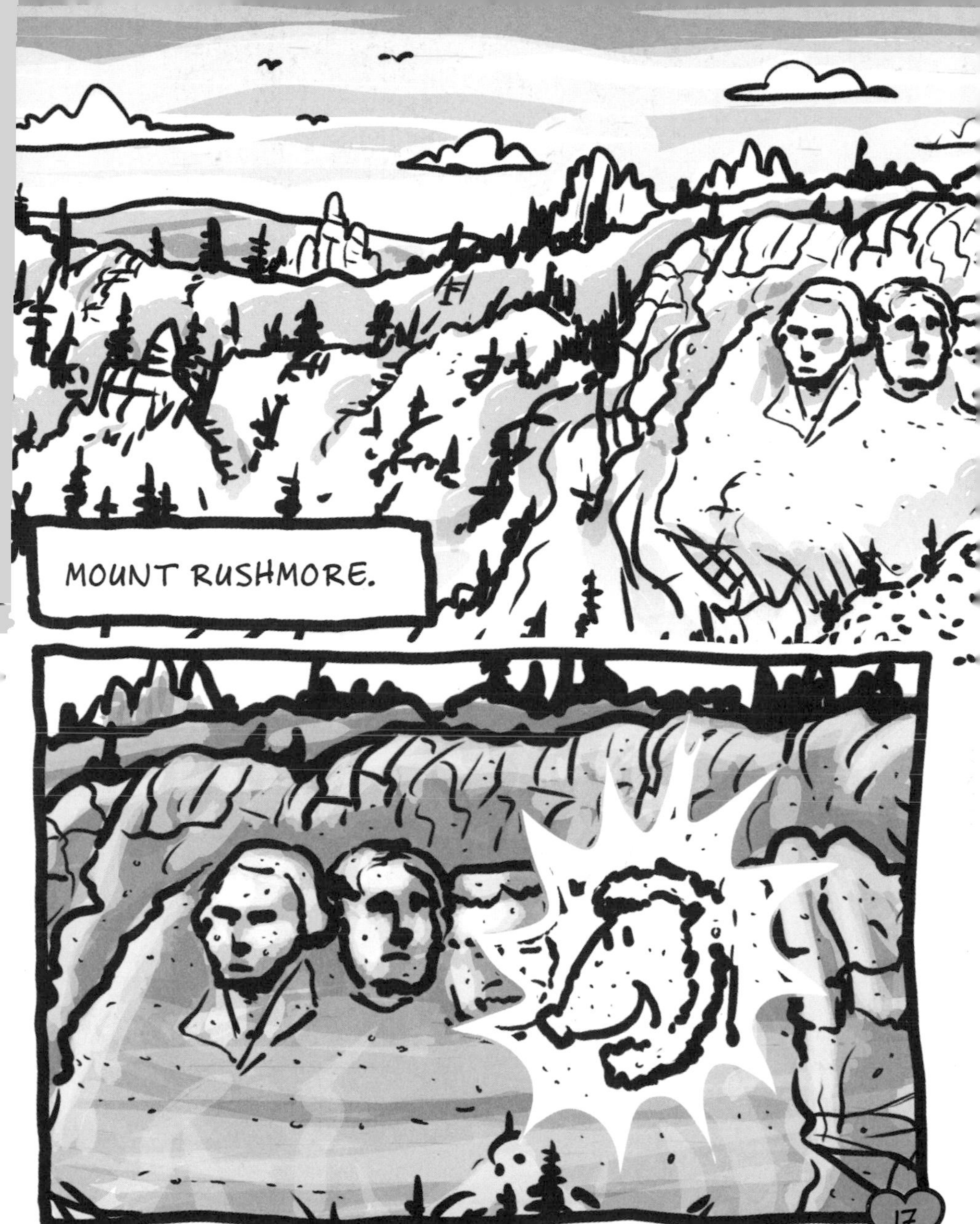
MOUNT RUSHMORE.

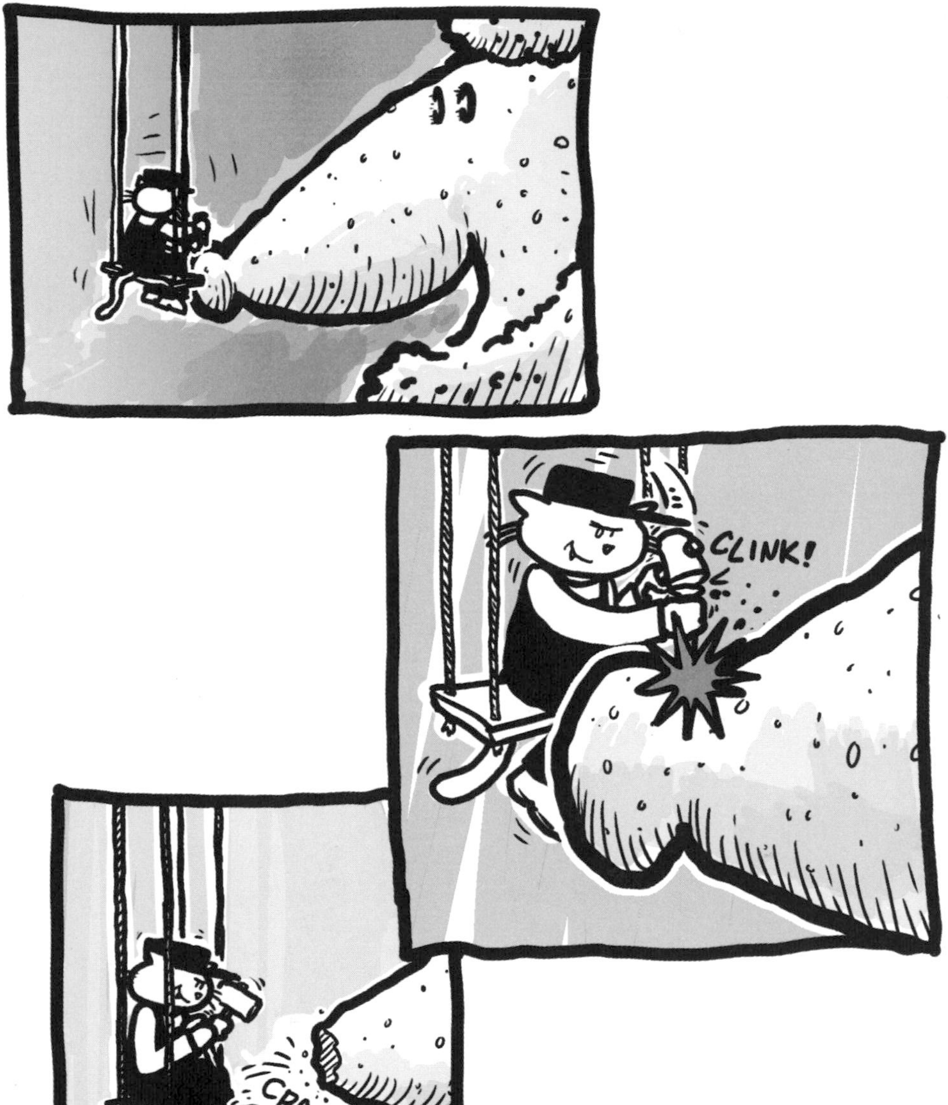
CLINK!
CRACK!

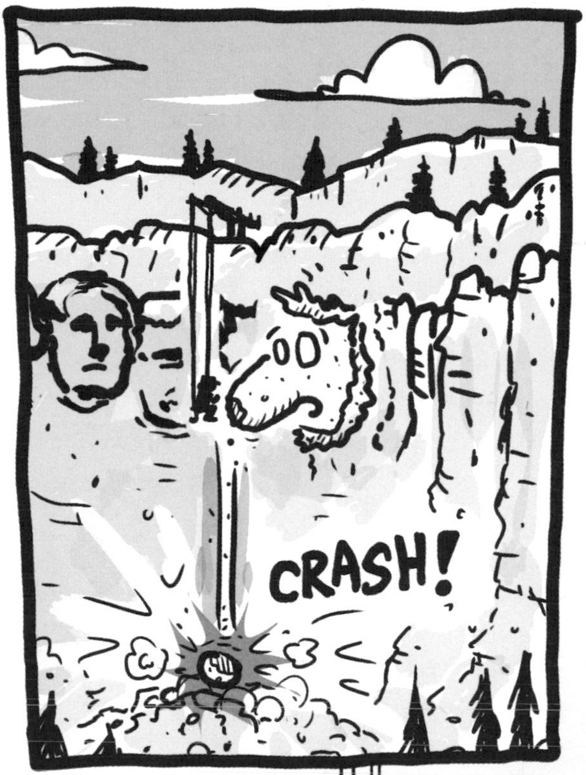
CRASH!

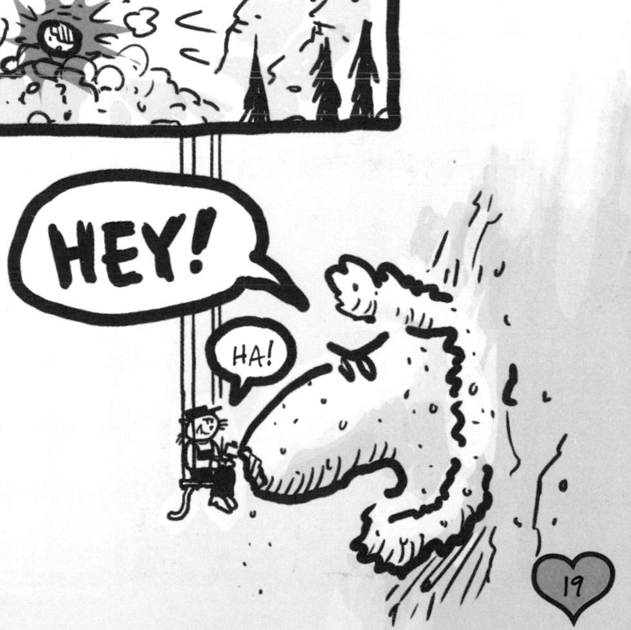
HEY!
HA!

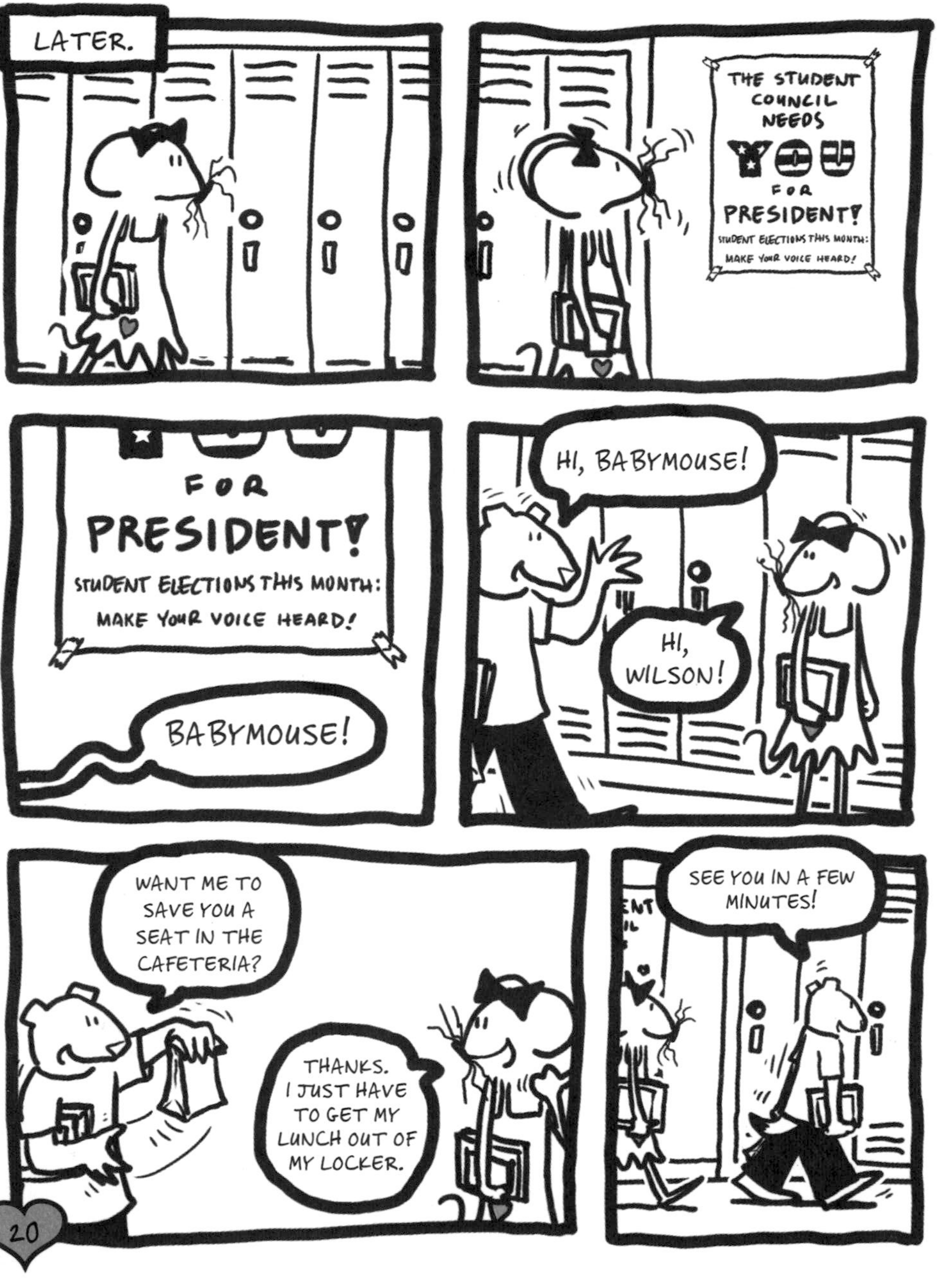
LATER.
THE STUDENT COUNCIL NEEDS YOU FOR PRESIDENT!
STUDENT ELECTIONS THIS MONTH: MAKE YOUR VOICE HEARD!
FOR PRESIDENT!
STUDENT ELECTIONS THIS MONTH:
MAKE YOUR VOICE HEARD!
BABYMOUSE!
HI, BABYMOUSE!
HI, WILSON!
WANT ME TO SAVE YOU A SEAT IN THE CAFETERIA?
THANKS. I JUST HAVE TO GET MY LUNCH OUT OF MY LOCKER.
SEE YOU IN A FEW MINUTES!

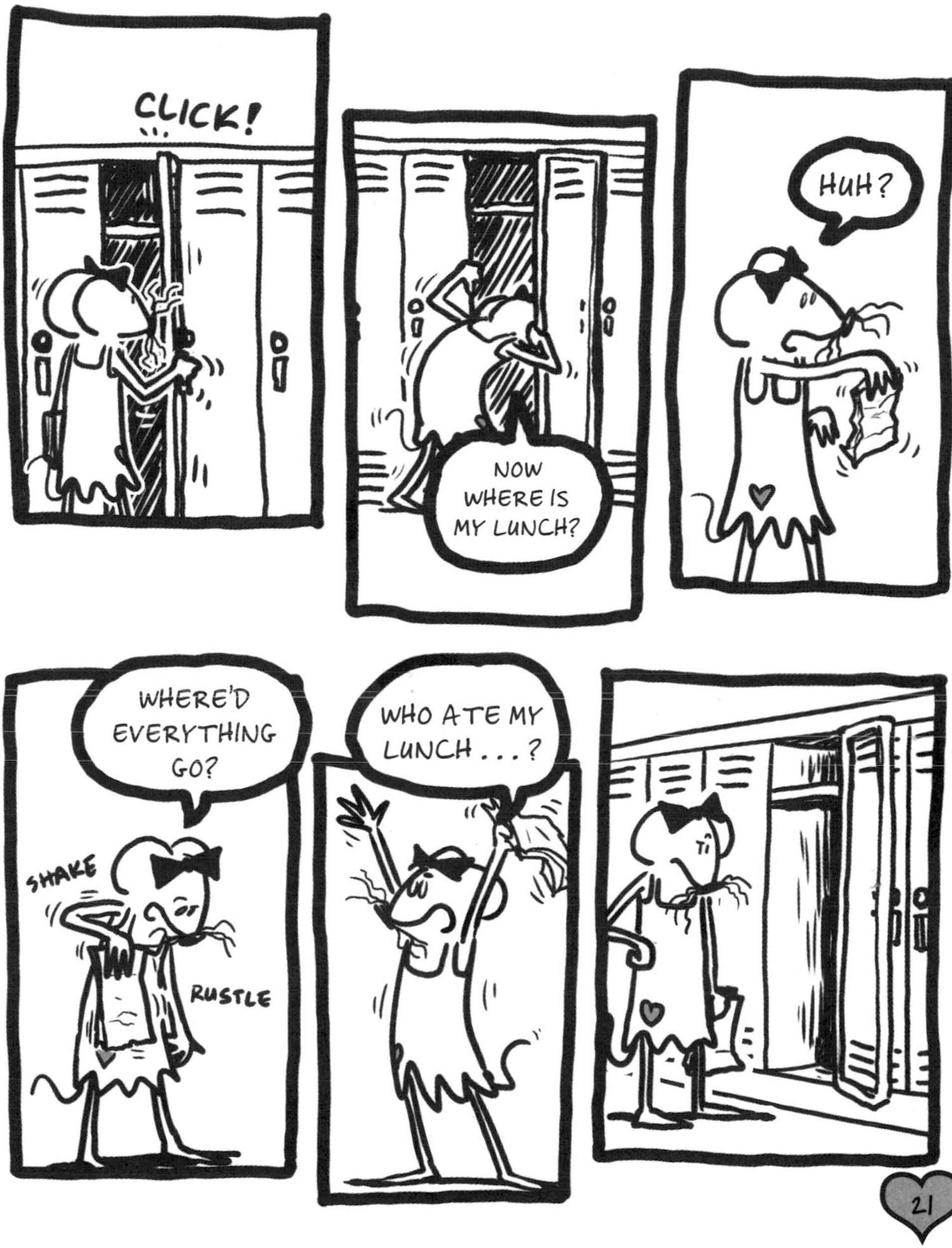
CLICK!
NOW WHERE IS MY LUNCH?
HUH?
WHERE'D EVERYTHING GO?
SHAKE
RUSTLE
WHO ATE MY LUNCH . . . ?

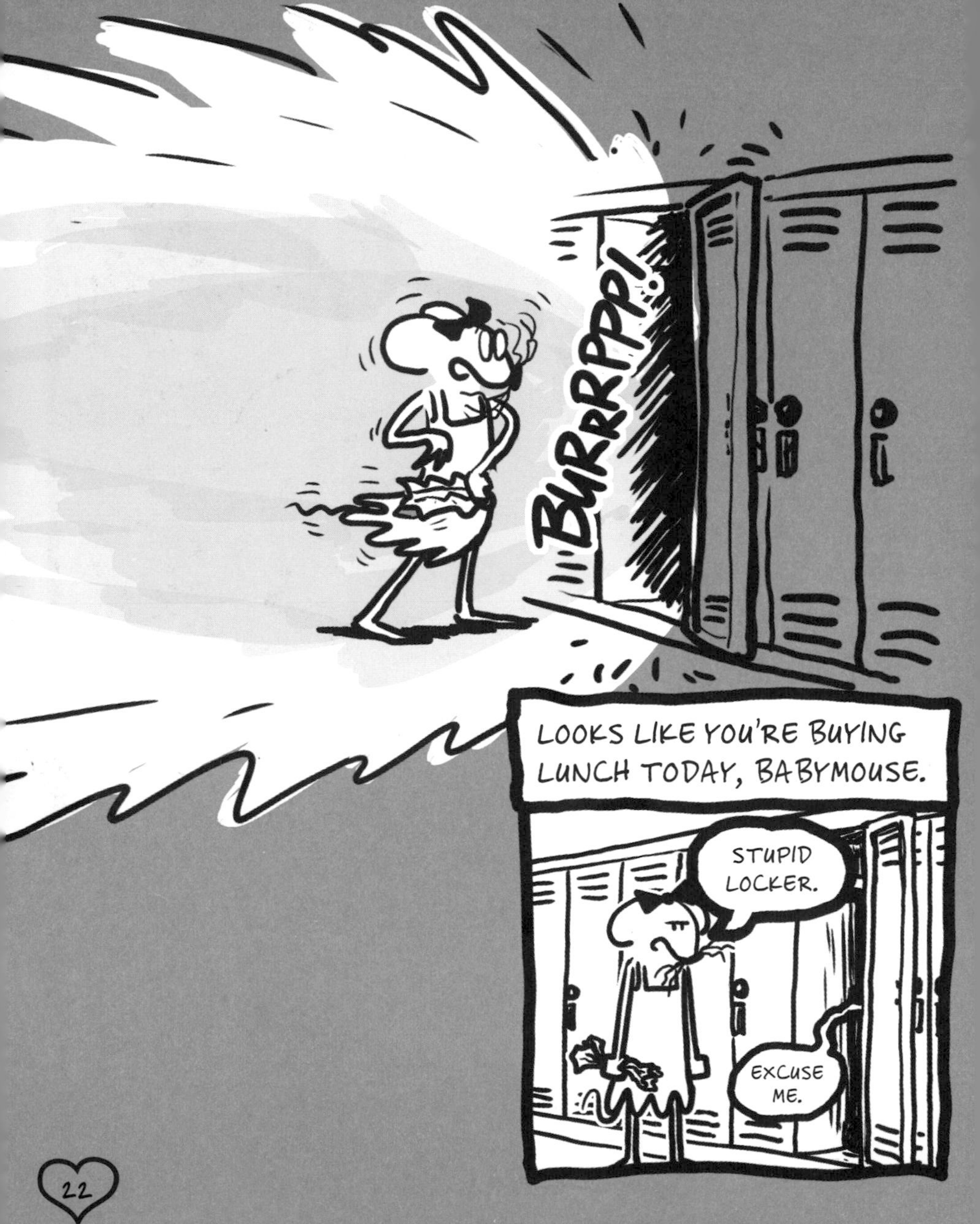
BURRRPPP!
LOOKS LIKE YOU'RE BUYING LUNCH TODAY, BABYMOUSE.
STUPID LOCKER.
EXCUSE ME.

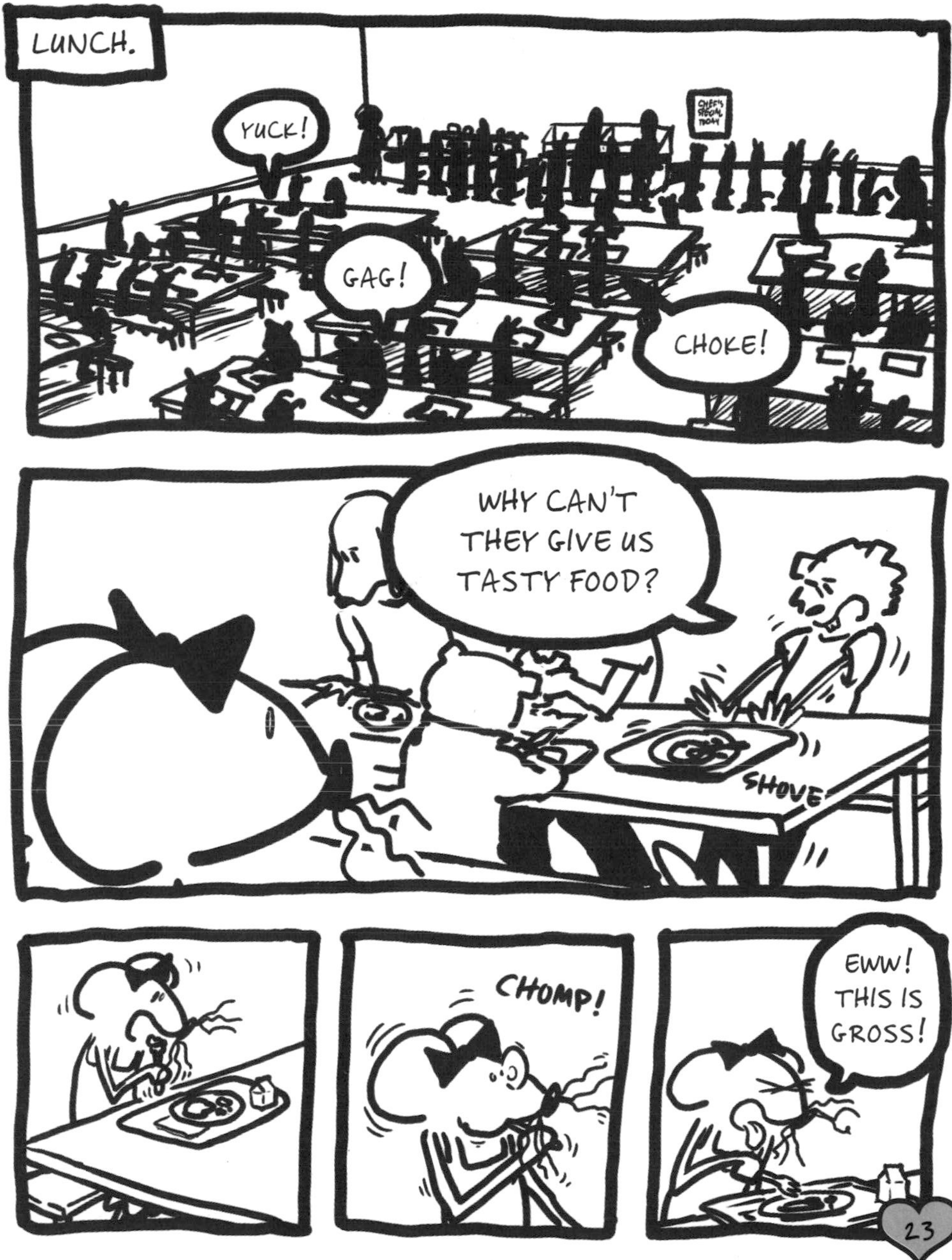
LUNCH.
YUCK!
GAG!
CHOKE!
WHY CAN'T THEY GIVE US TASTY FOOD?
SHOVE
CHOMP!
EWW! THIS IS GROSS!

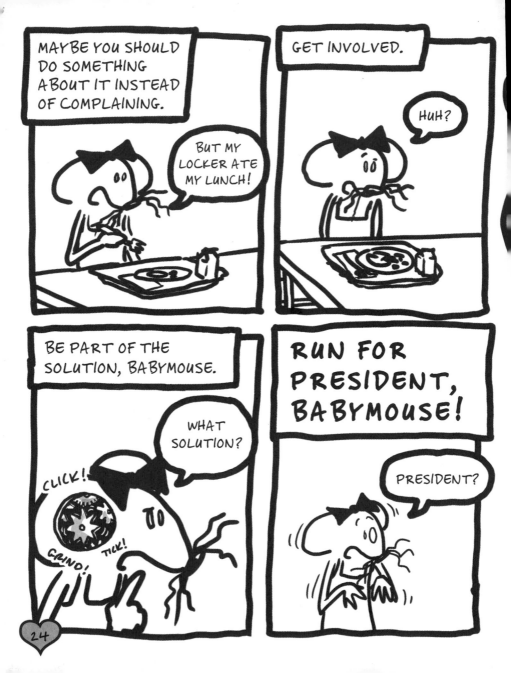

24

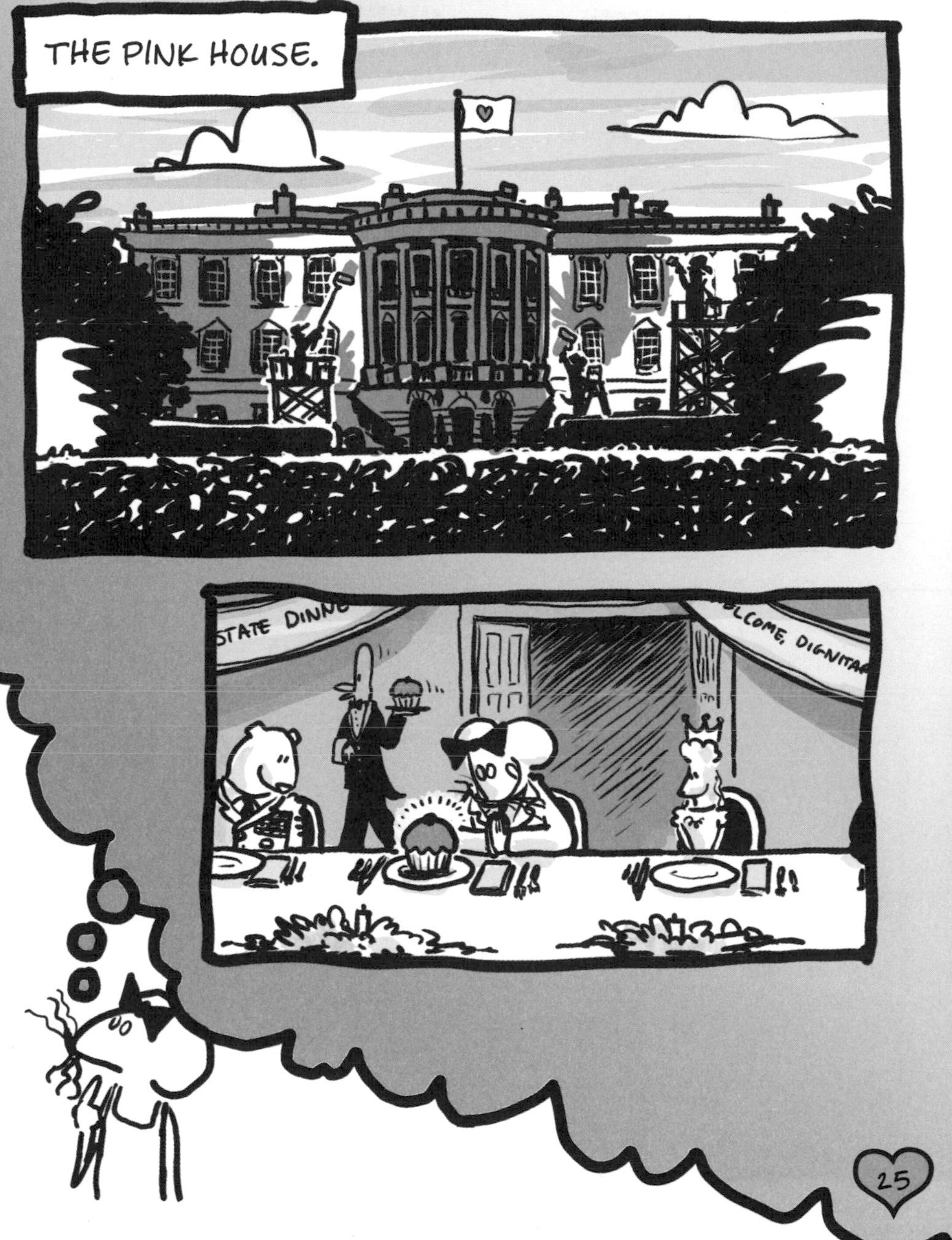
THE PINK HOUSE.
STATE DINNE
LCOME, DIGNITAR

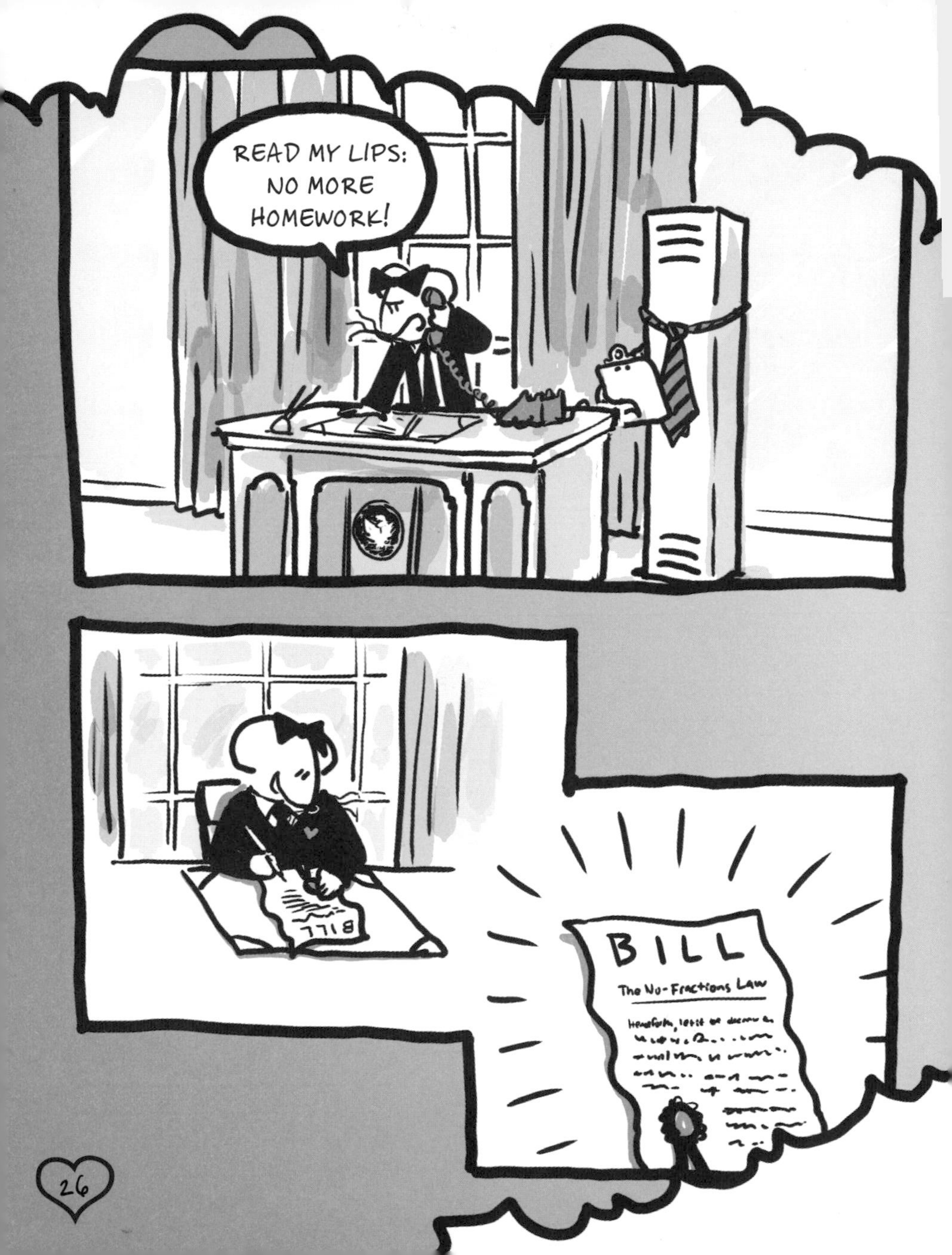
READ MY LIPS: NO MORE HOMEWORK!
BILL
The No-Fractions Law

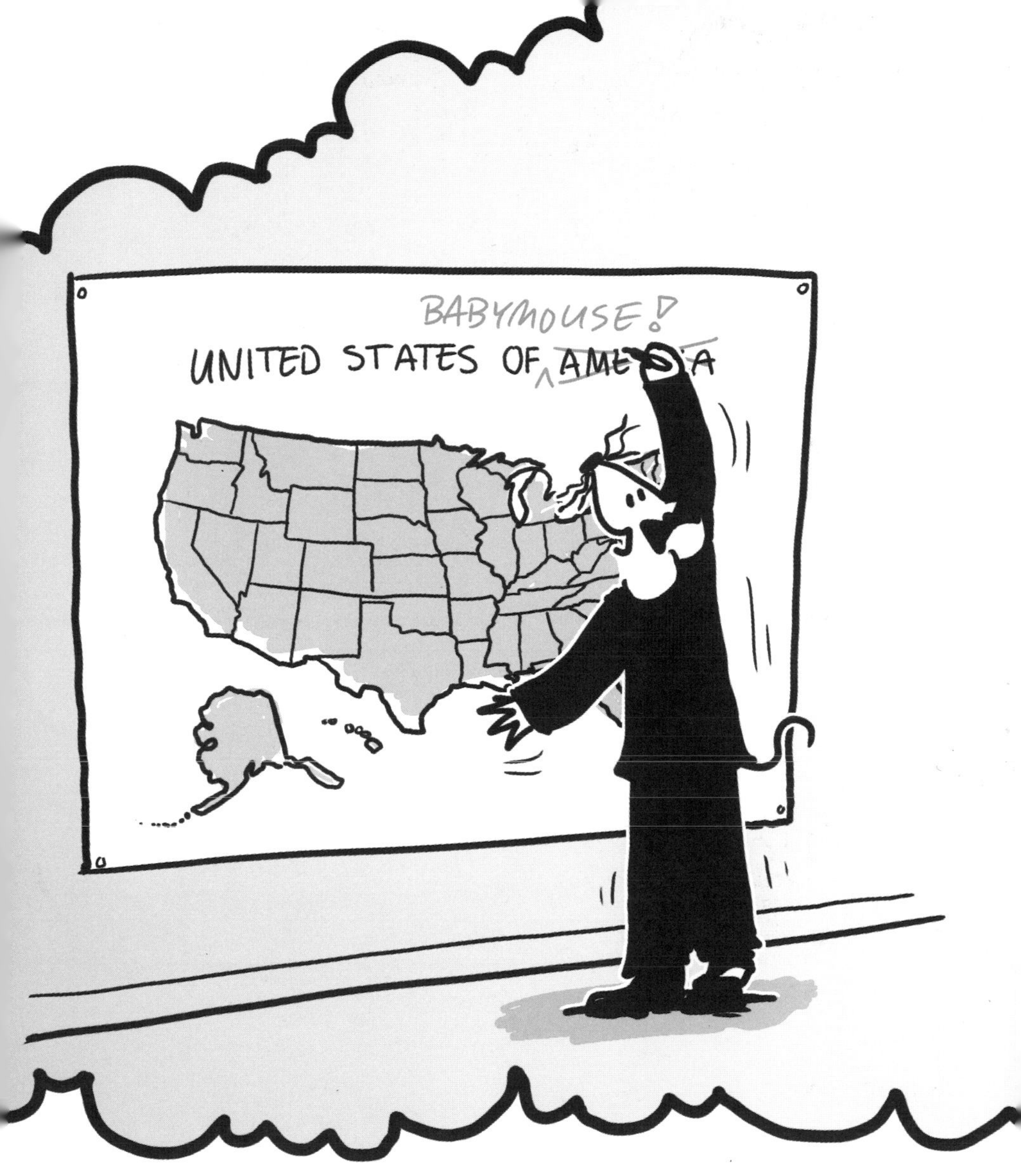
BABYMOUSE!
UNITED STATES OF AME A

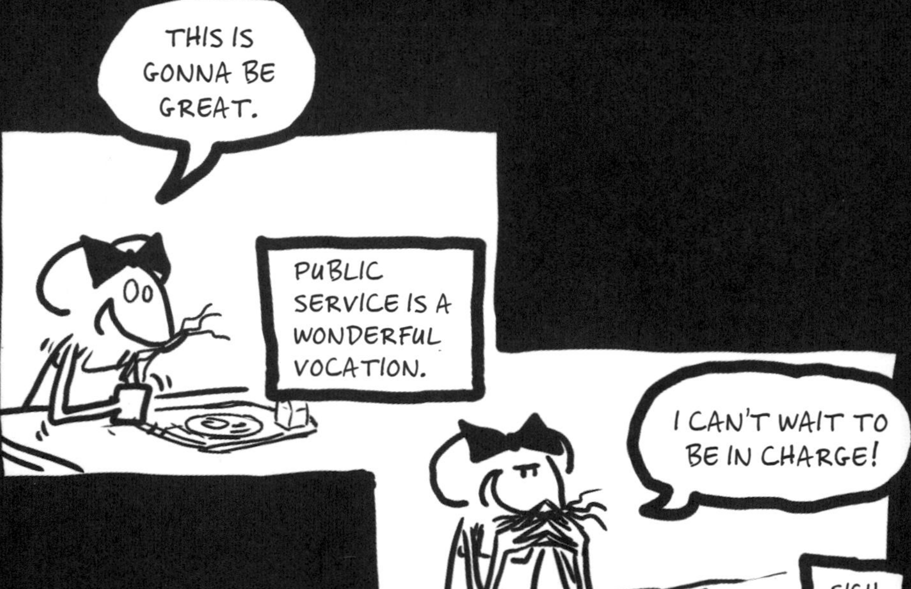
THIS IS GONNA BE GREAT.
PUBLIC SERVICE IS A WONDERFUL VOCATION.
I CAN'T WAIT TO BE IN CHARGE!
SIGH.

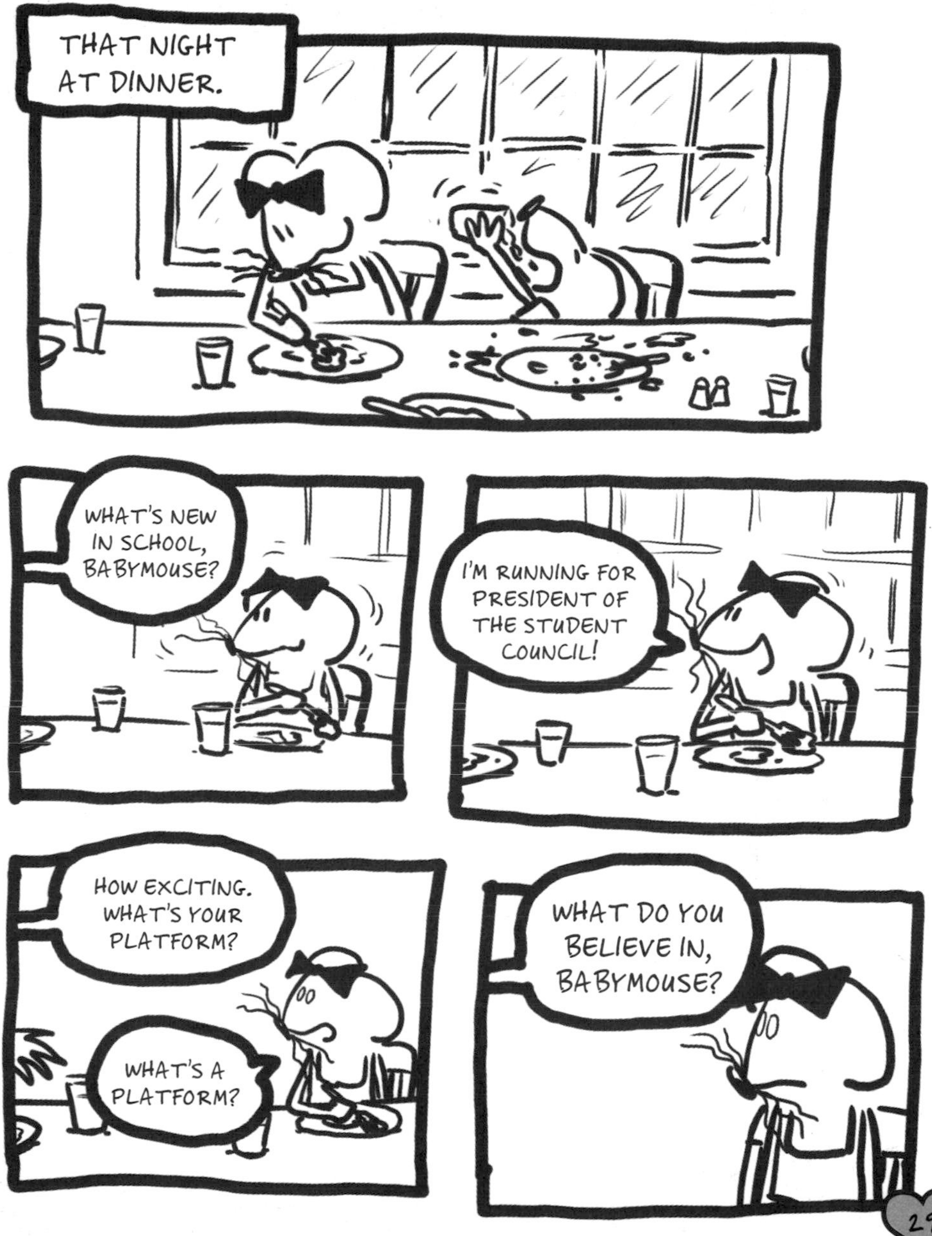
THAT NIGHT AT DINNER.
WHAT'S NEW IN SCHOOL, BABYMOUSE?
I'M RUNNING FOR PRESIDENT OF THE STUDENT COUNCIL!
HOW EXCITING. WHAT'S YOUR PLATFORM?
WHAT'S A PLATFORM?
WHAT DO YOU BELIEVE IN, BABYMOUSE?

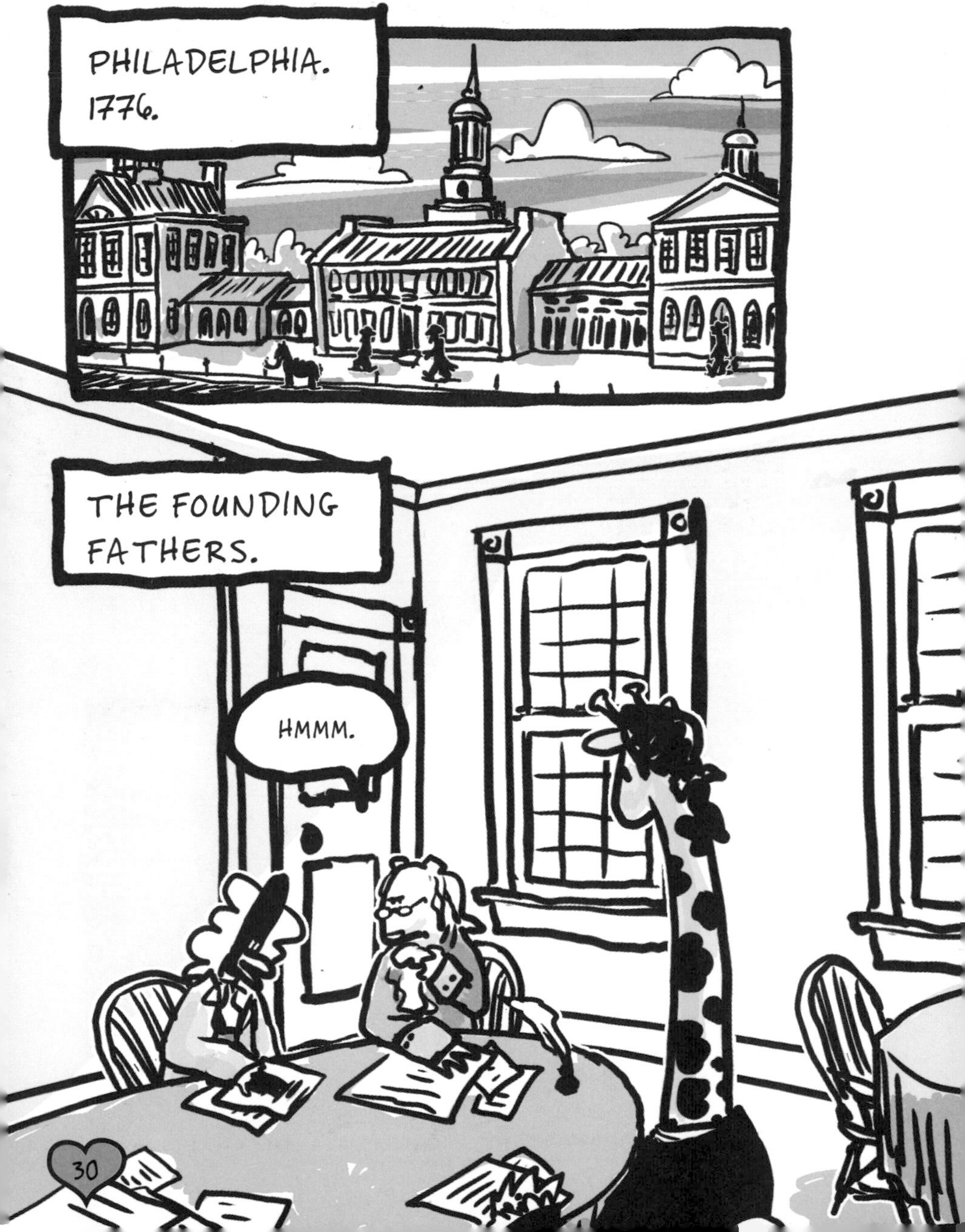
PHILADELPHIA.
1776.
THE FOUNDING FATHERS.
HMMM.

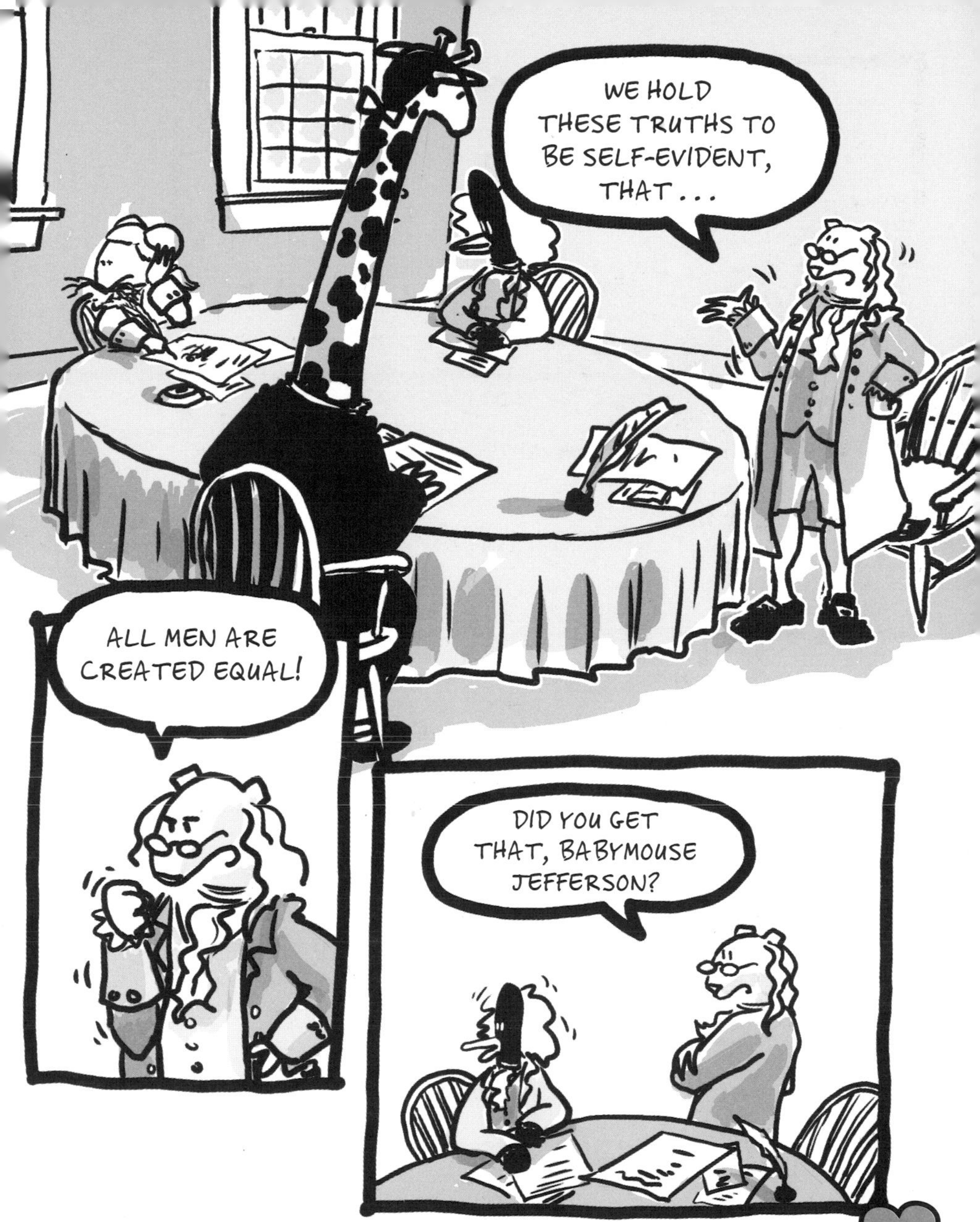
WE HOLD THESE TRUTHS TO BE SELF-EVIDENT, THAT . . .
ALL MEN ARE CREATED EQUAL!
DID YOU GET THAT, BABYMOUSE JEFFERSON?

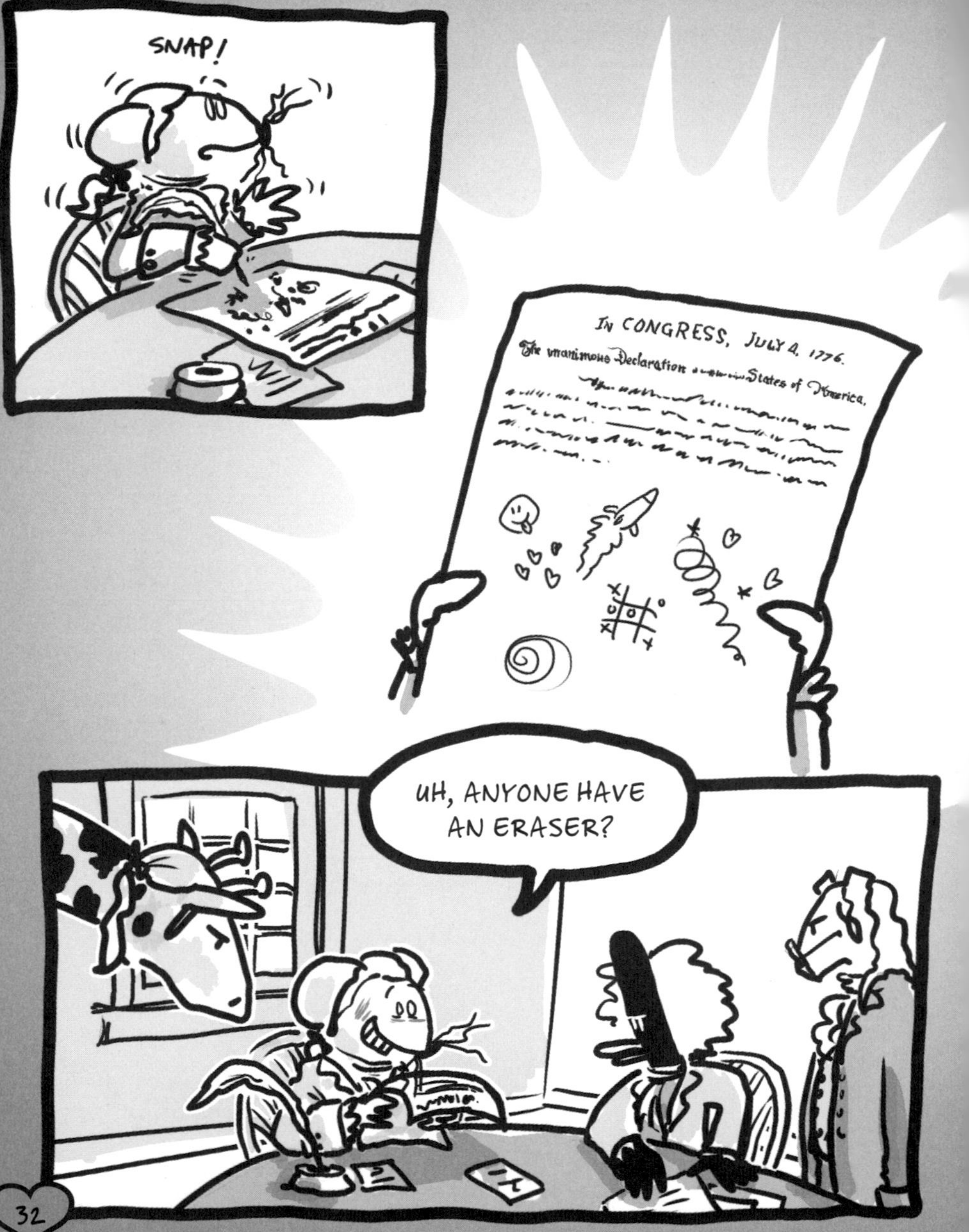
SNAP!
IN CONGRESS, JULY 4, 1776.
The unanimous Declaration States of America.
UH, ANYONE HAVE AN ERASER?

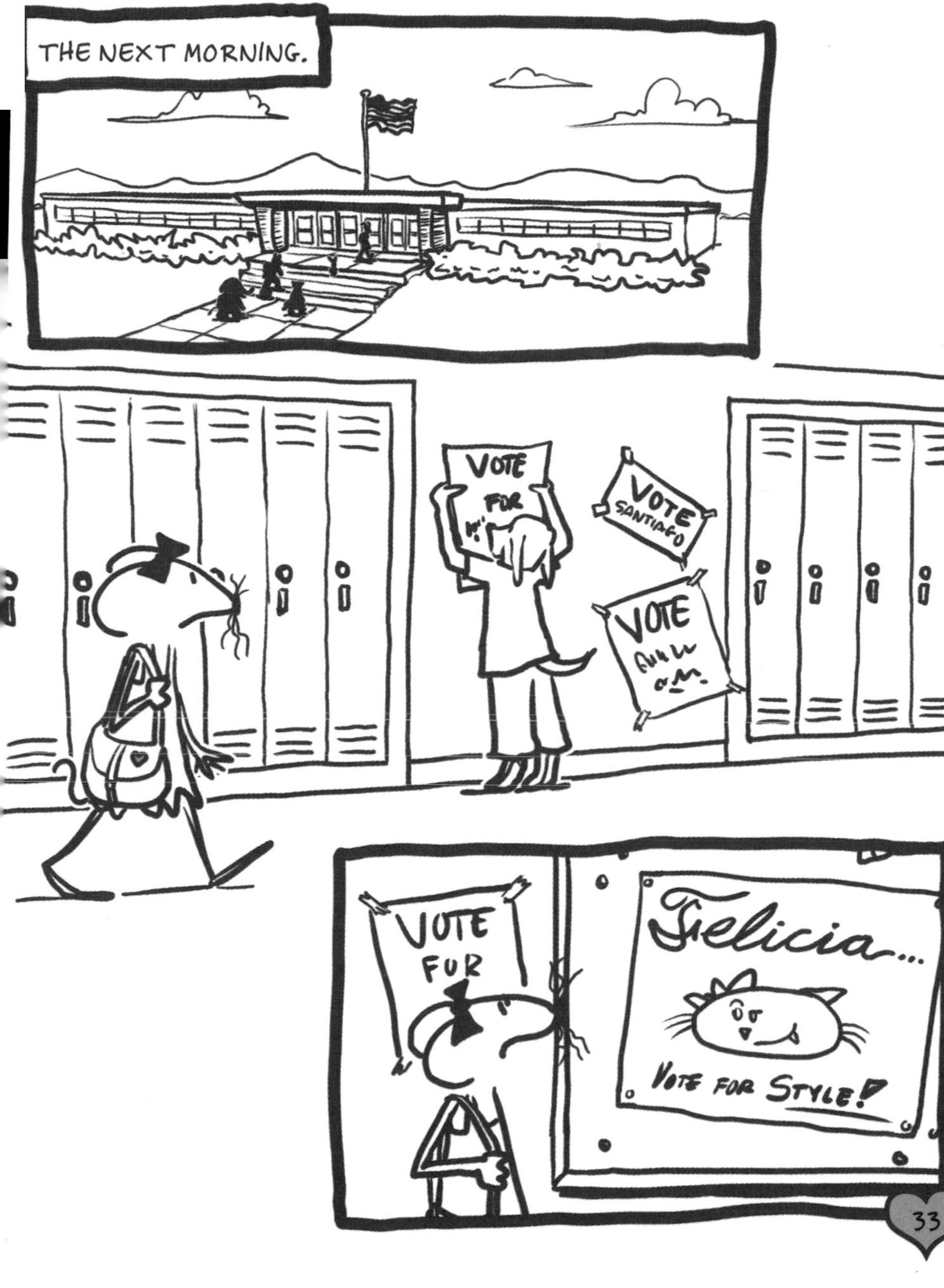
THE NEXT MORNING.
VOTE
VOTE SANTIAGO
VOTE
VOTE FUR
Felicia...
VOTE FOR STYLE!

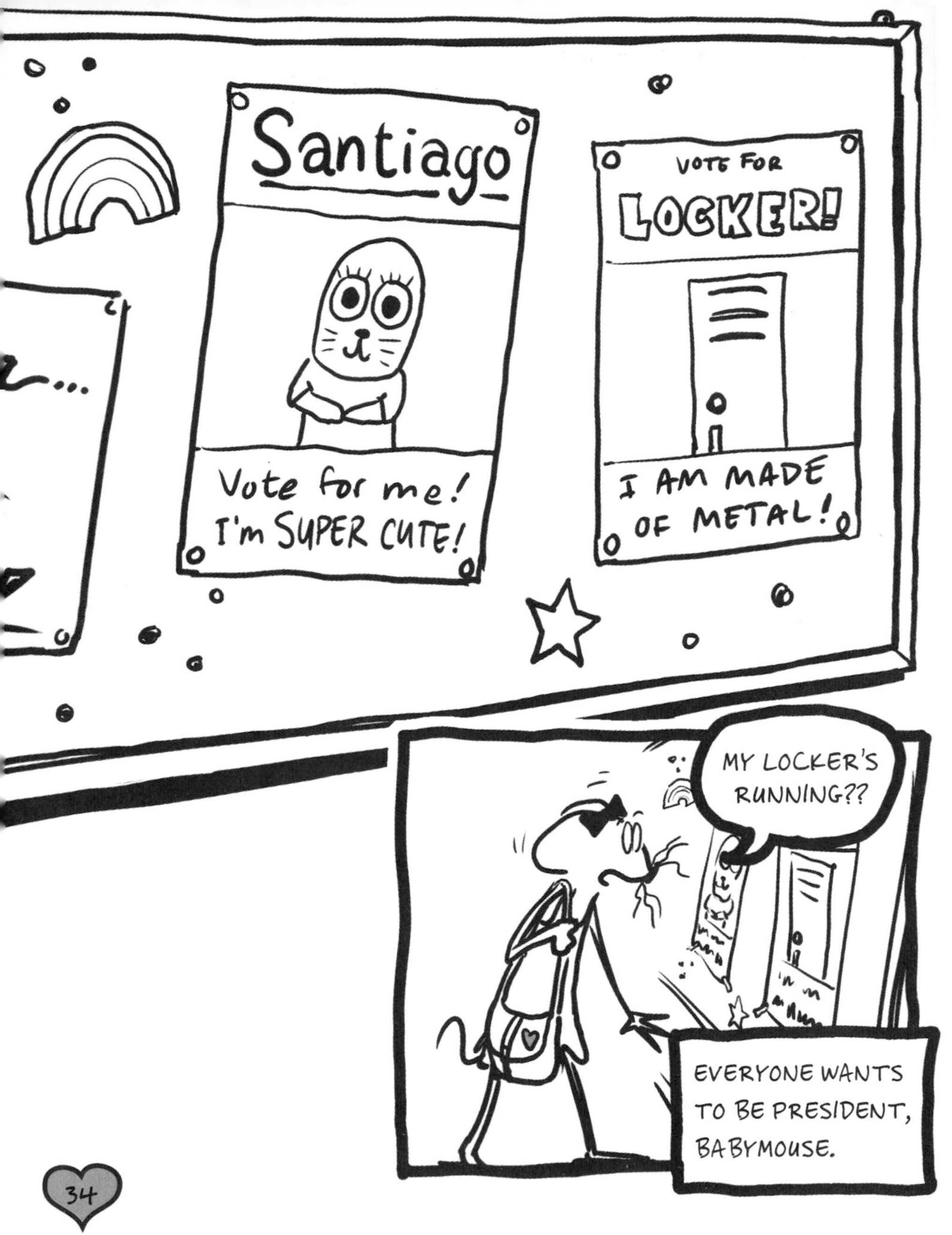
Santiago
Vote for me! I'm SUPER CUTE!
VOTE FOR
LOCKER!
I AM MADE OF METAL!
MY LOCKER'S RUNNING??
EVERYONE WANTS TO BE PRESIDENT, BABYMOUSE.

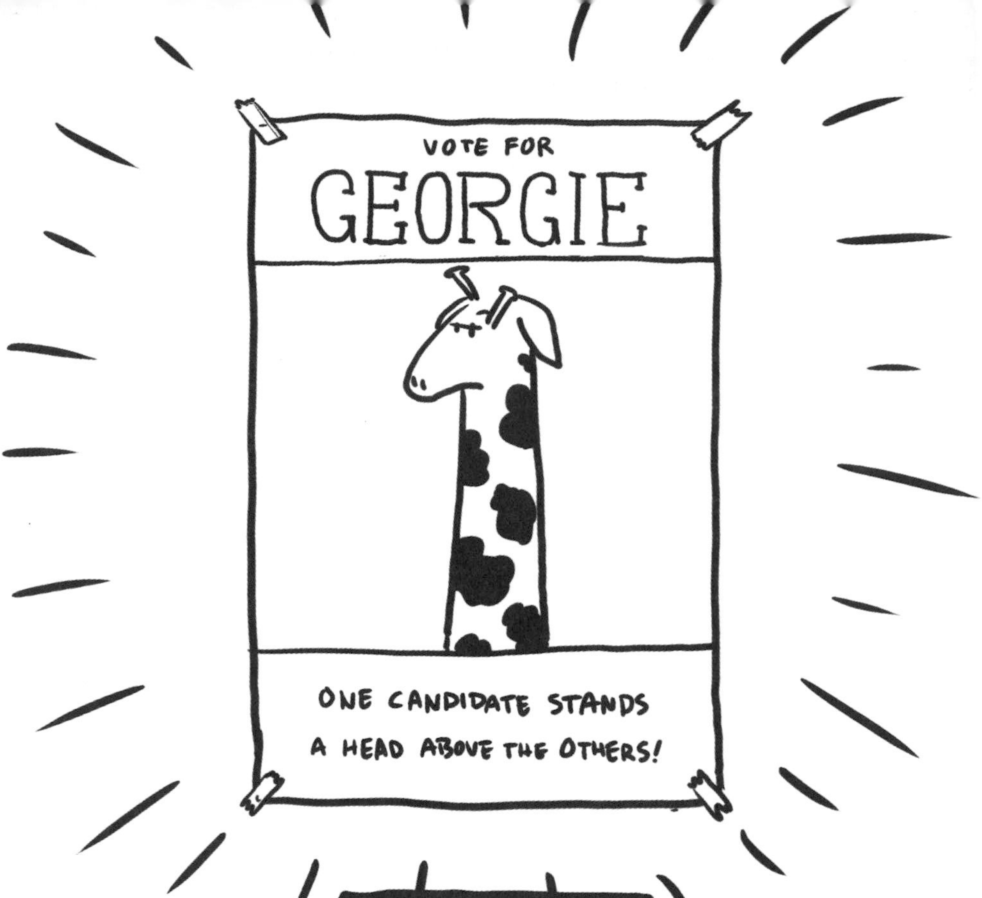
VOTE FOR
GEORGIE
ONE CANDIDATE STANDS
A HEAD ABOVE THE OTHERS!

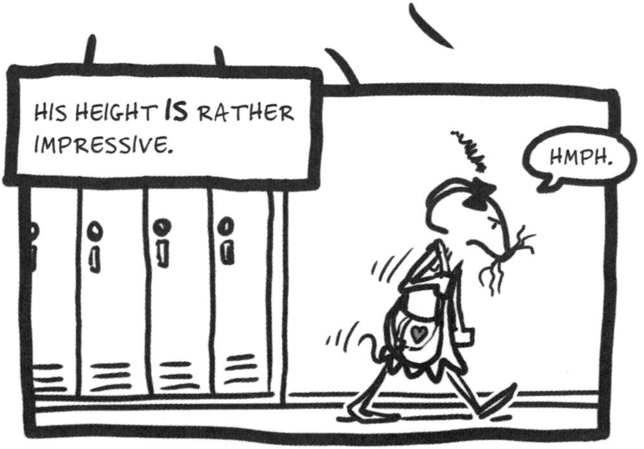
HIS HEIGHT **IS** RATHER IMPRESSIVE.
HMPH.

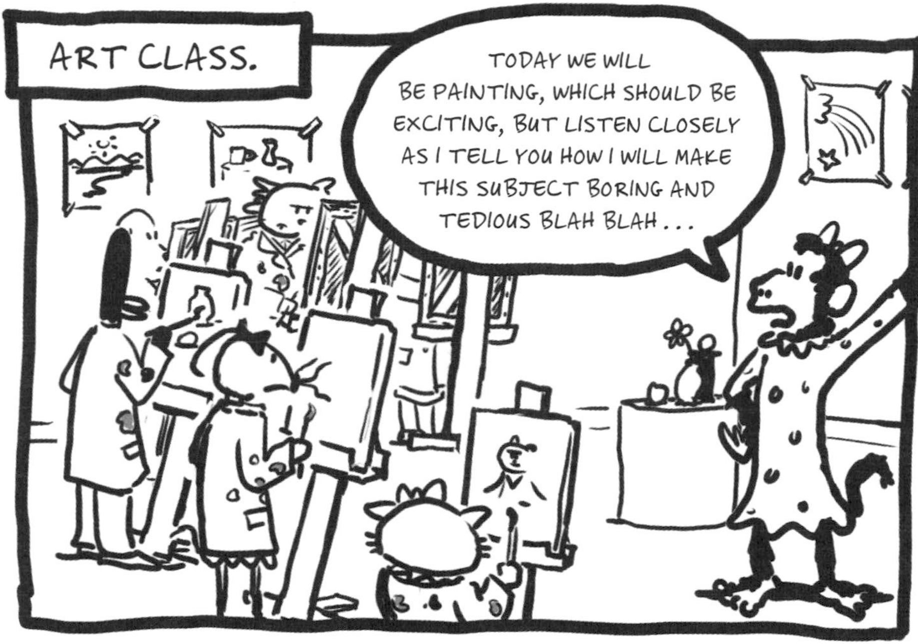
ART CLASS.
TODAY WE WILL BE PAINTING, WHICH SHOULD BE EXCITING, BUT LISTEN CLOSELY AS I TELL YOU HOW I WILL MAKE THIS SUBJECT BORING AND TEDIOUS BLAH BLAH . . .

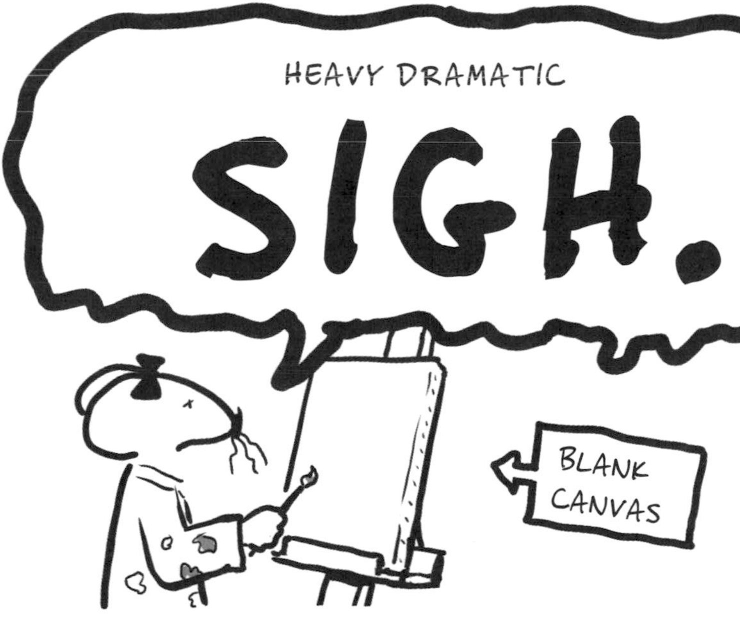
HEAVY DRAMATIC
SIGH.
BLANK CANVAS

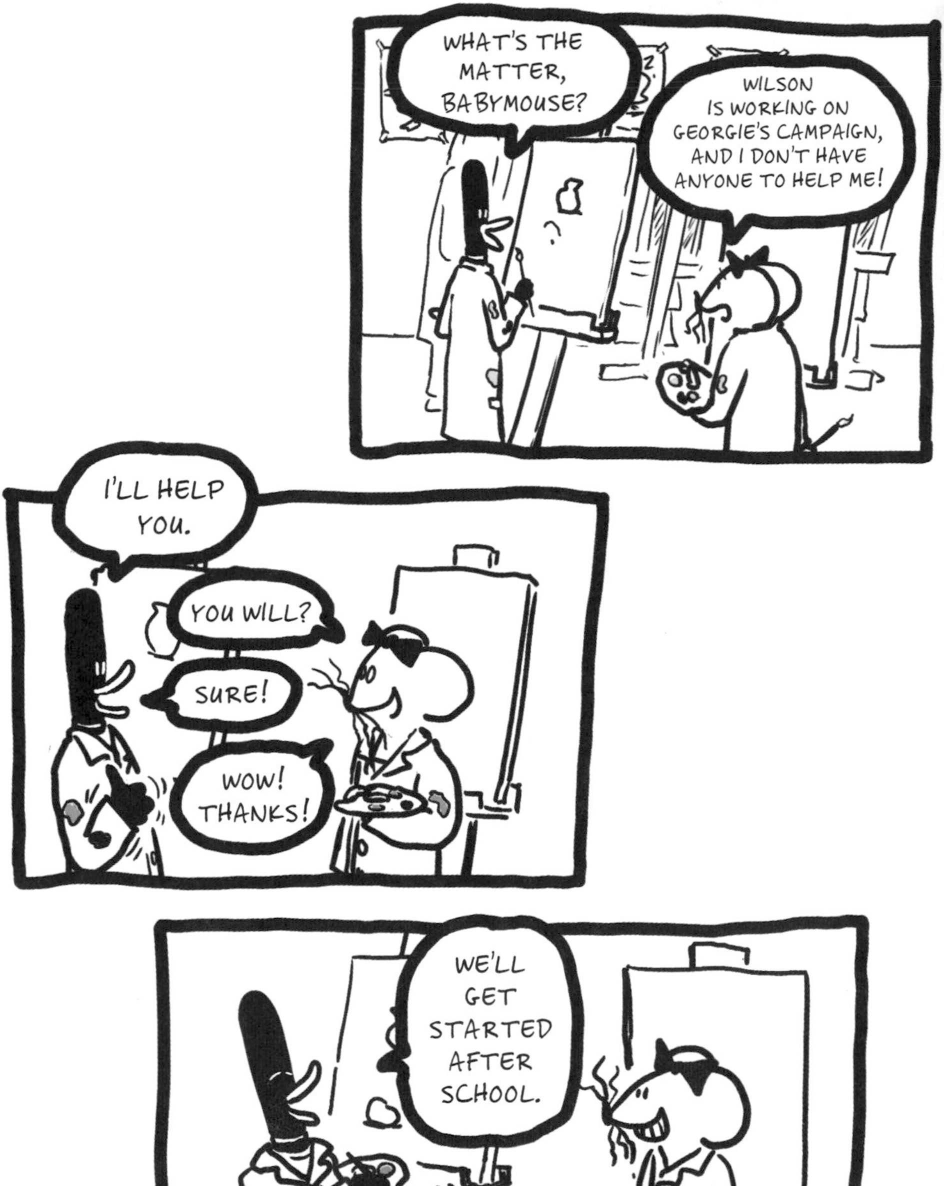
WHAT'S THE MATTER, BABYMOUSE?
WILSON IS WORKING ON GEORGIE'S CAMPAIGN, AND I DON'T HAVE ANYONE TO HELP ME!
I'LL HELP YOU.
YOU WILL?
SURE!
WOW! THANKS!
WE'LL GET STARTED AFTER SCHOOL.

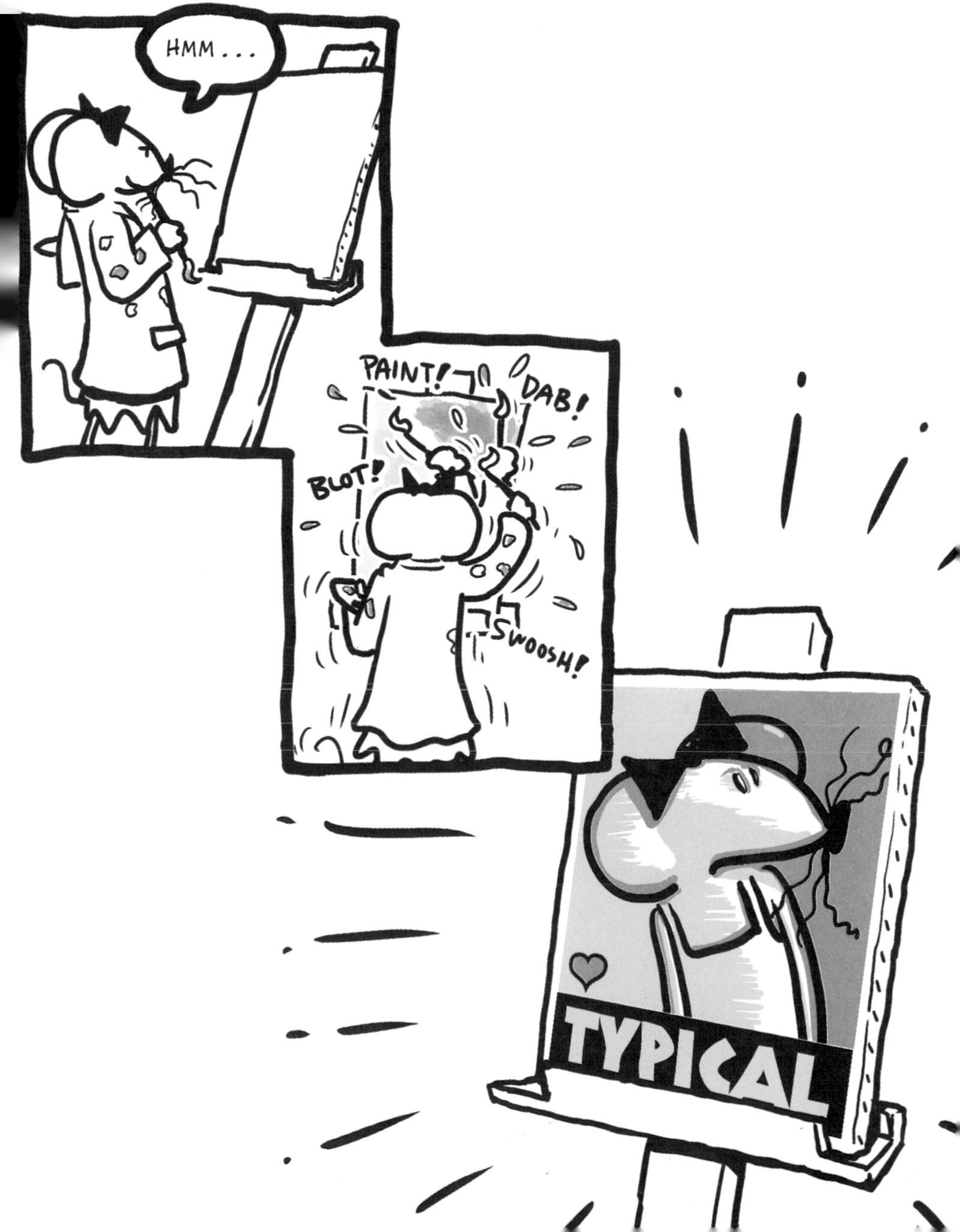
HMM...
PAINT!
DAB!
BLOT!
SWOOSH!
TYPICAL

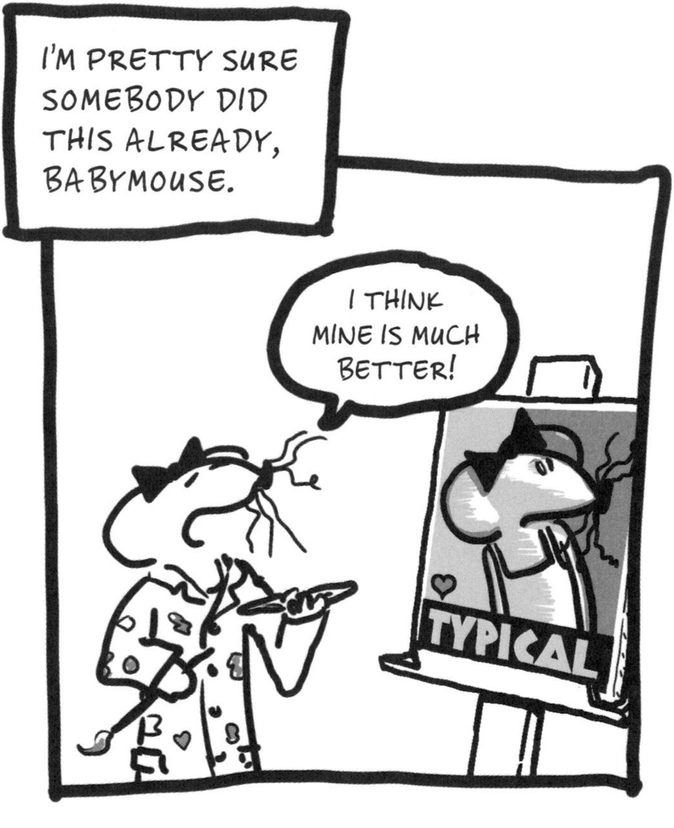
I'M PRETTY SURE SOMEBODY DID THIS ALREADY, BABYMOUSE.
I THINK MINE IS MUCH BETTER!
TYPICAL

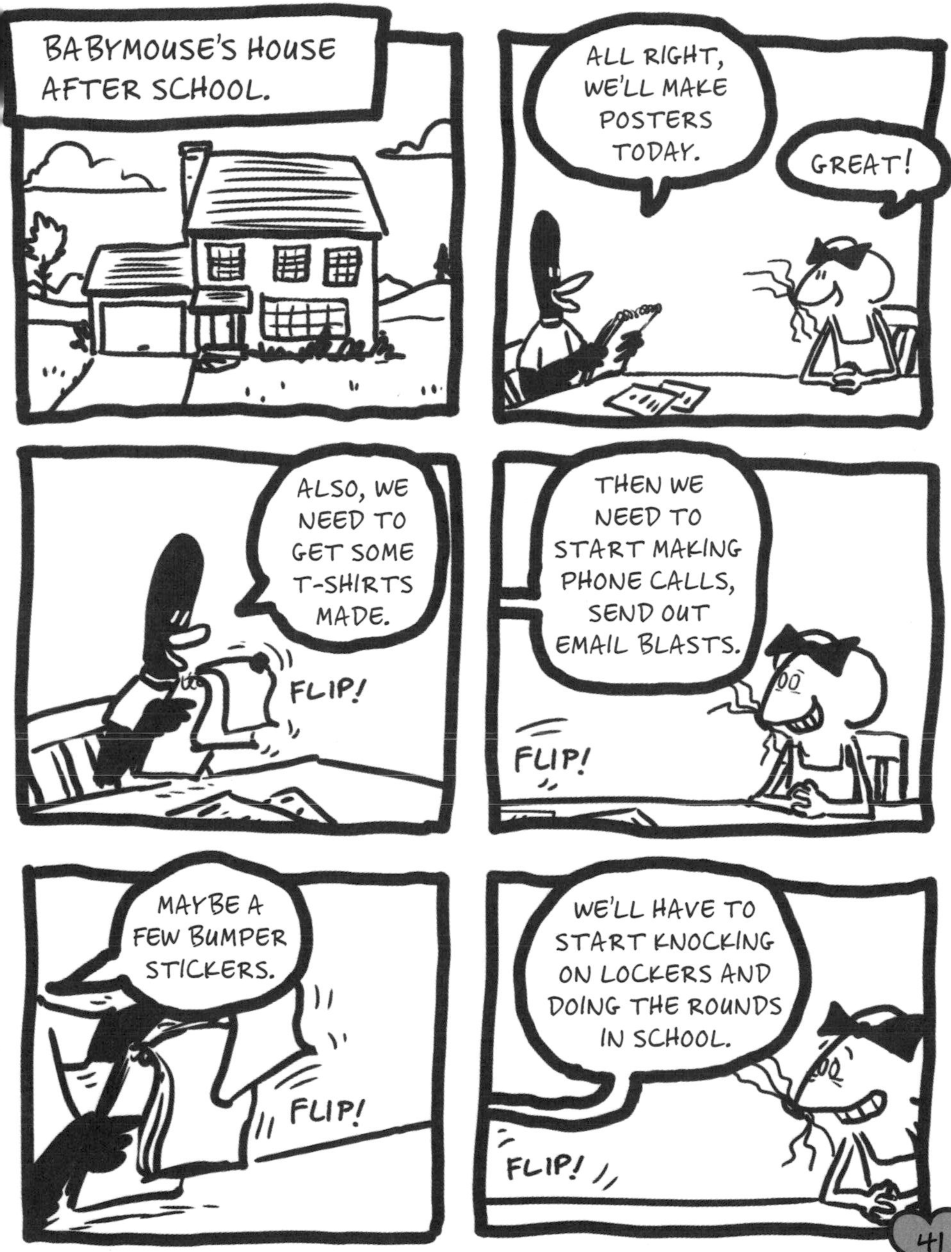
BABYMOUSE'S HOUSE AFTER SCHOOL.
ALL RIGHT, WE'LL MAKE POSTERS TODAY.
GREAT!
ALSO, WE NEED TO GET SOME T-SHIRTS MADE.
FLIP!
THEN WE NEED TO START MAKING PHONE CALLS, SEND OUT EMAIL BLASTS.
FLIP!
MAYBE A FEW BUMPER STICKERS.
FLIP!
WE'LL HAVE TO START KNOCKING ON LOCKERS AND DOING THE ROUNDS IN SCHOOL.
FLIP!

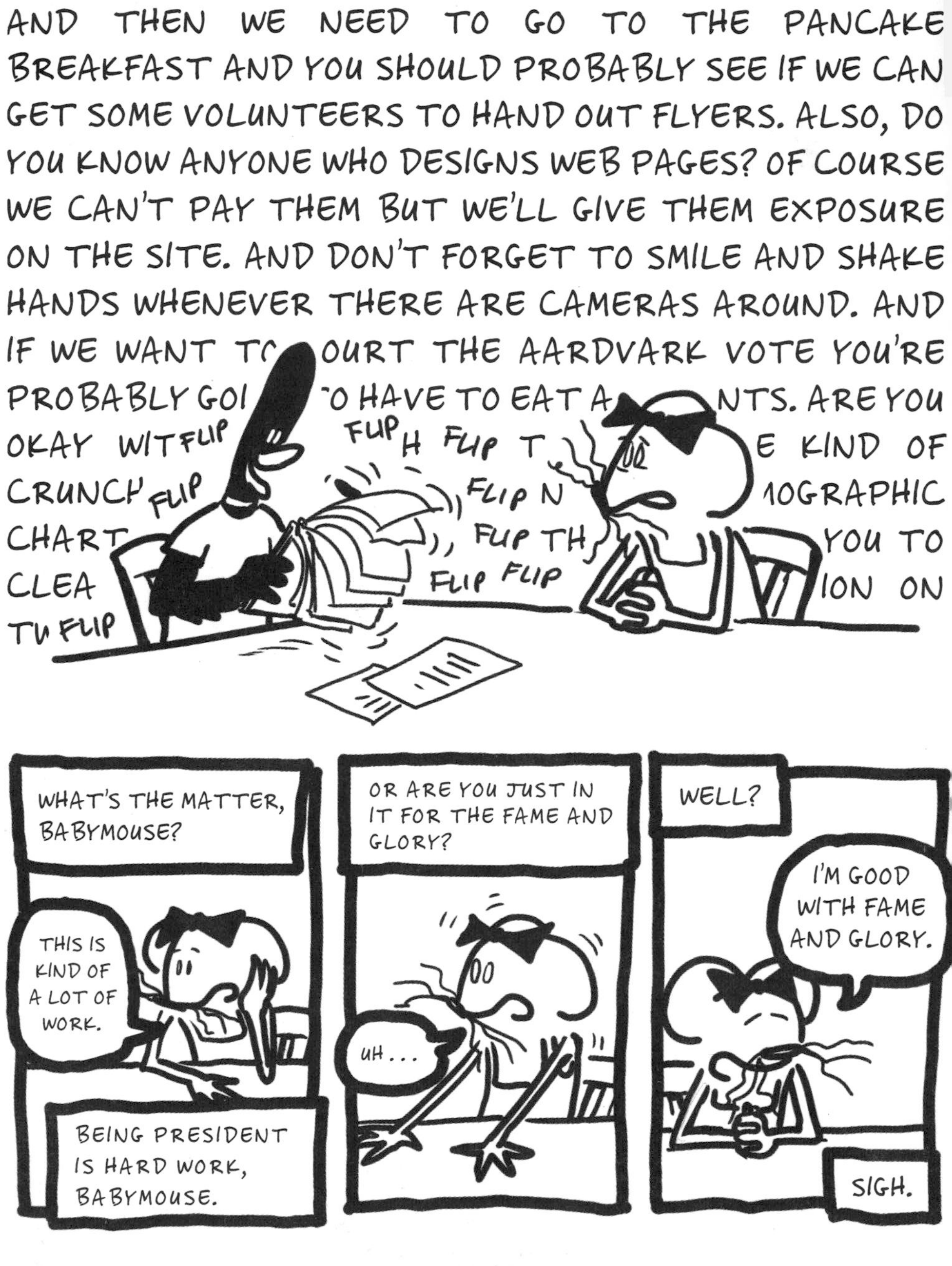

AND THEN WE NEED TO GO TO THE PANCAKE BREAKFAST AND YOU SHOULD PROBABLY SEE IF WE CAN GET SOME VOLUNTEERS TO HAND OUT FLYERS. ALSO, DO YOU KNOW ANYONE WHO DESIGNS WEB PAGES? OF COURSE WE CAN'T PAY THEM BUT WE'LL GIVE THEM EXPOSURE ON THE SITE. AND DON'T FORGET TO SMILE AND SHAKE HANDS WHENEVER THERE ARE CAMERAS AROUND. AND IF WE WANT TO COURT THE AARDVARK VOTE YOU'RE PROBABLY GOI TO HAVE TO EAT A NTS. ARE YOU OKAY WIT H T E KIND OF CRUNCH N 10GRAPHIC CHART TH YOU TO CLEA ION ON TU
FLIP FLIP FLIP FLIP FLIP FLIP FLIP FLIP FLIP
WHAT'S THE MATTER, BABYMOUSE?
THIS IS KIND OF A LOT OF WORK.
BEING PRESIDENT IS HARD WORK, BABYMOUSE.
OR ARE YOU JUST IN IT FOR THE FAME AND GLORY?
UH . . .
WELL?
I'M GOOD WITH FAME AND GLORY.
SIGH.

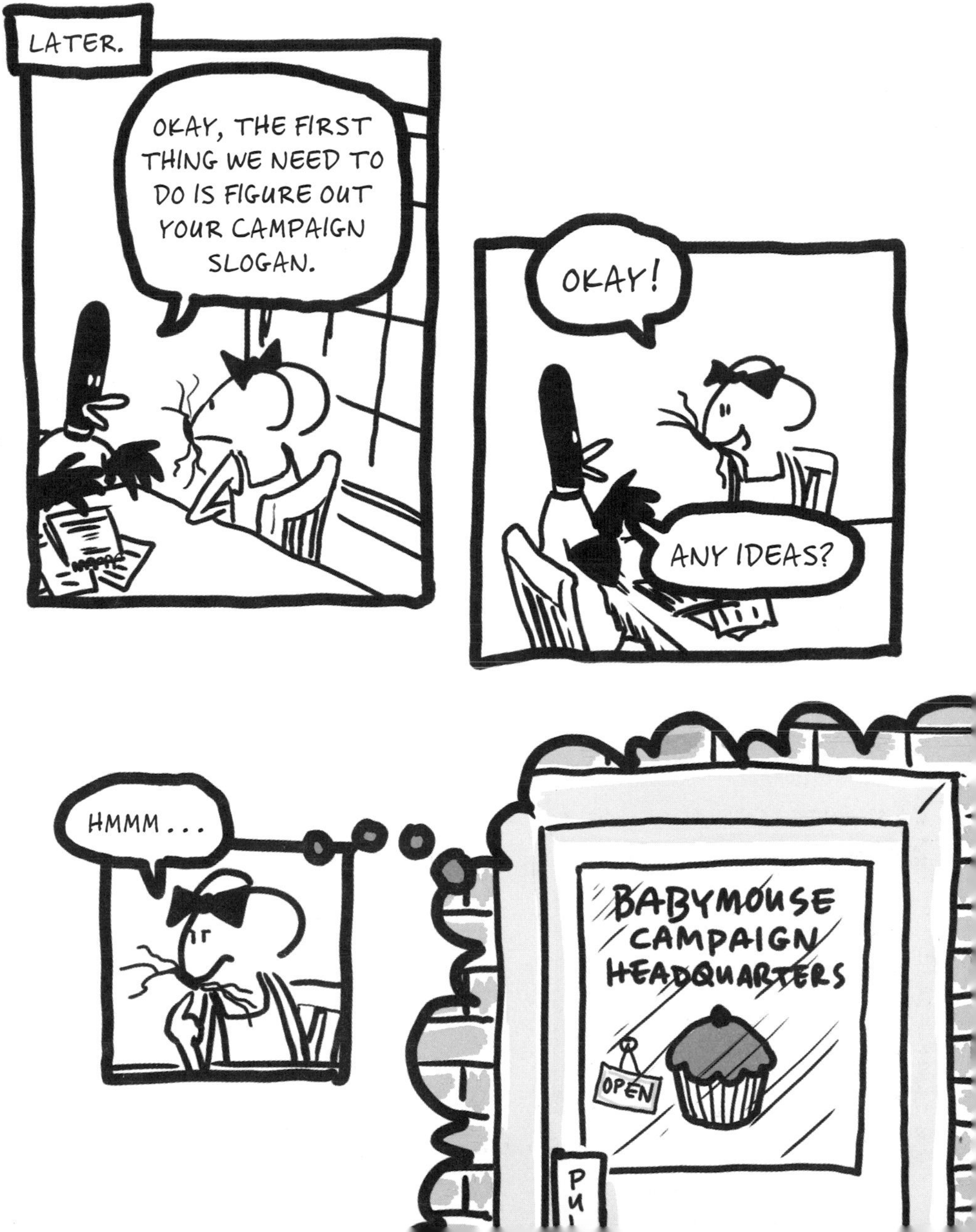
LATER.
OKAY, THE FIRST THING WE NEED TO DO IS FIGURE OUT YOUR CAMPAIGN SLOGAN.
OKAY!
ANY IDEAS?
HMMM...
BABYMOUSE CAMPAIGN HEADQUARTERS
OPEN

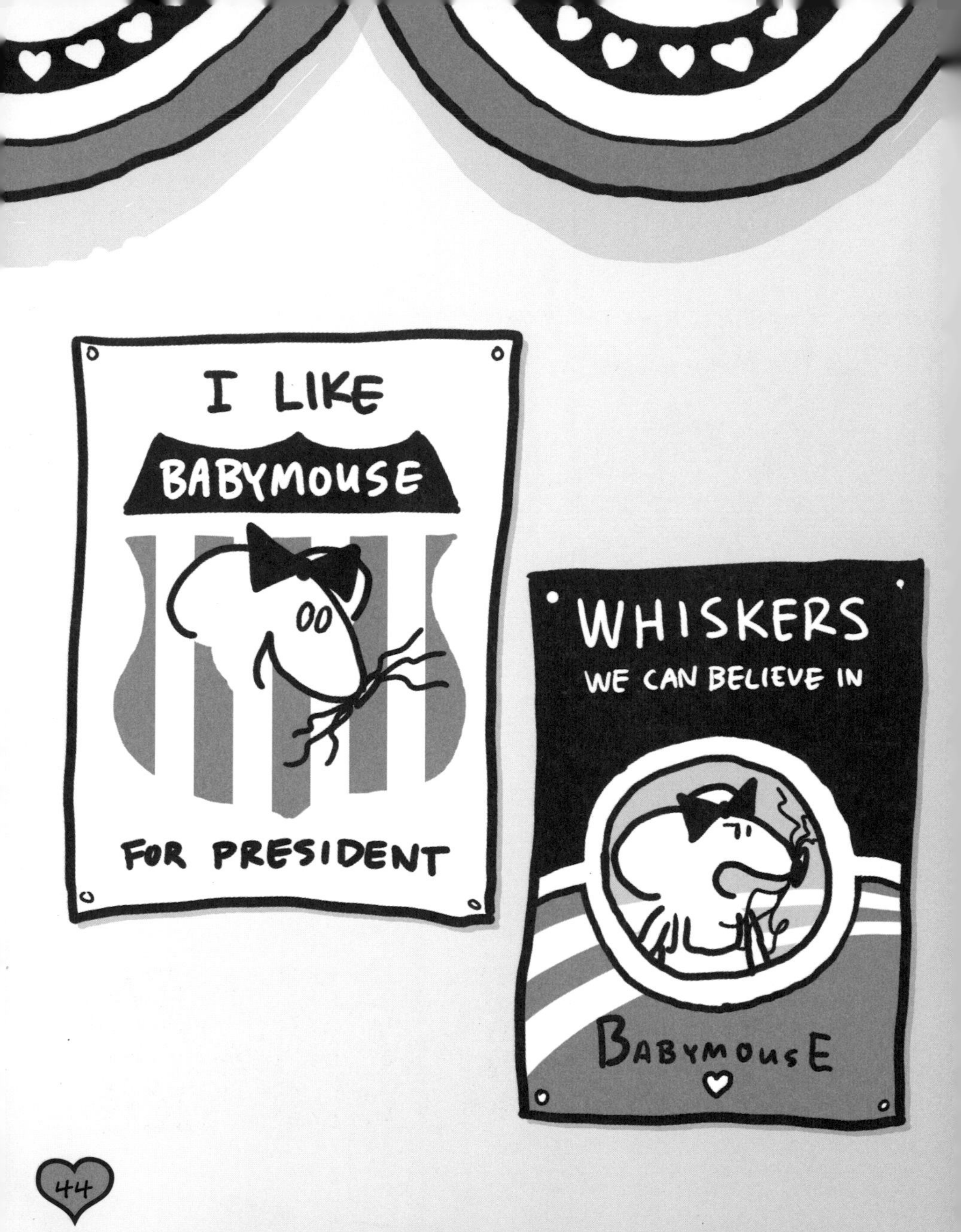
I LIKE
BABYMOUSE
FOR PRESIDENT
WHISKERS
WE CAN BELIEVE IN
BABYMOUSE

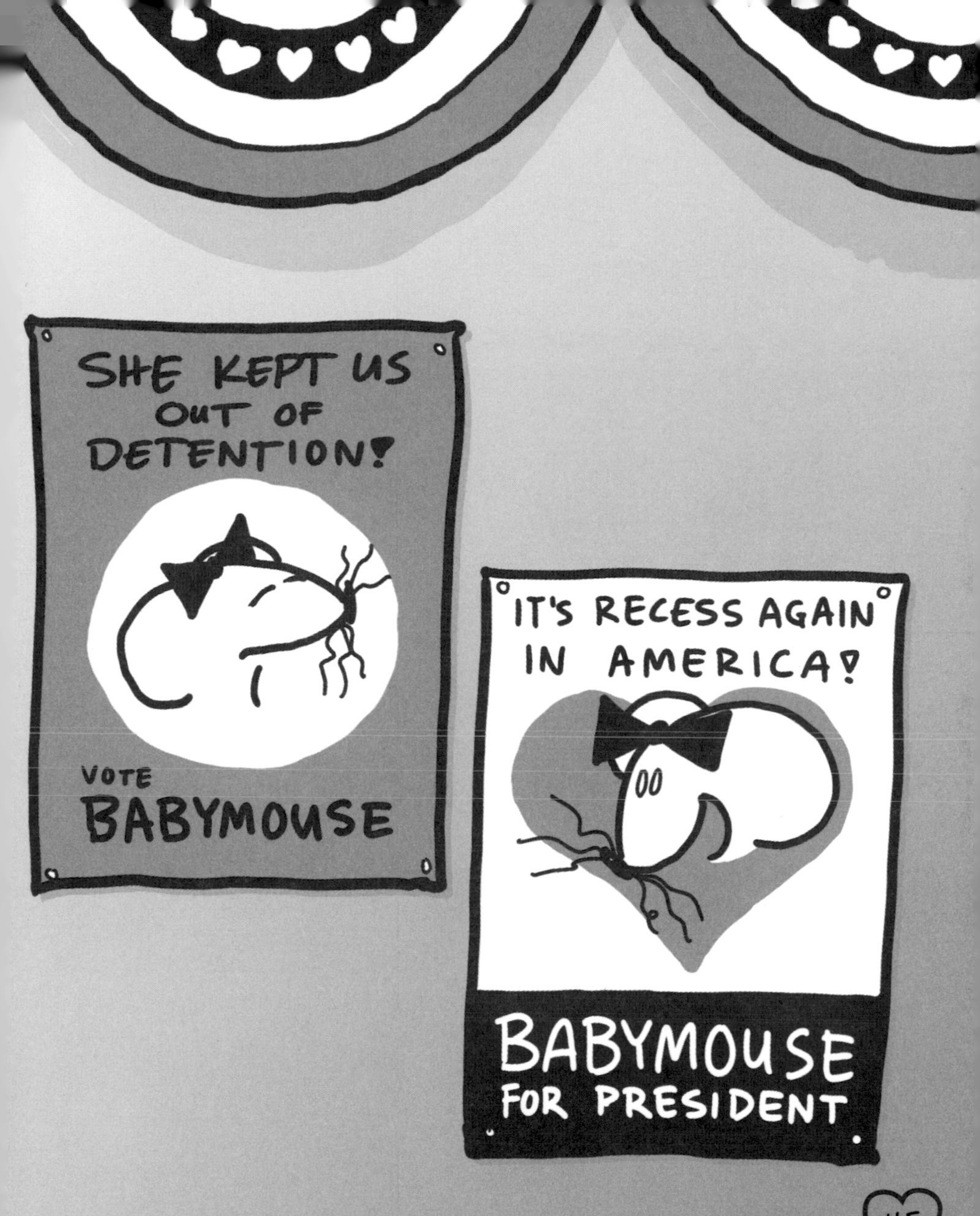

SHE KEPT US OUT OF DETENTION!
VOTE BABYMOUSE
IT'S RECESS AGAIN IN AMERICA!
BABYMOUSE FOR PRESIDENT

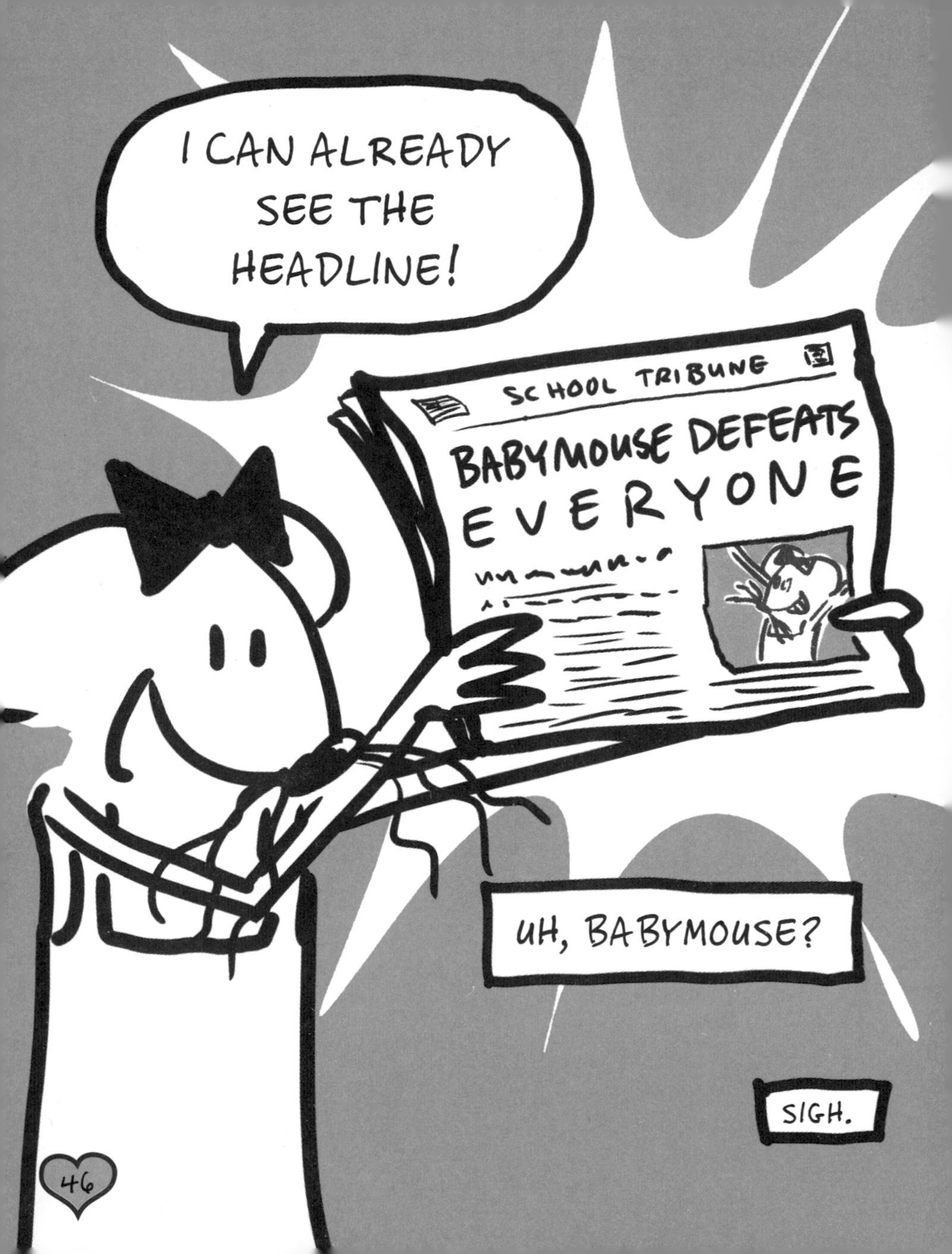
I CAN ALREADY SEE THE HEADLINE!
SCHOOL TRIBUNE
BABYMOUSE DEFEATS EVERYONE
UH, BABYMOUSE?
SIGH.

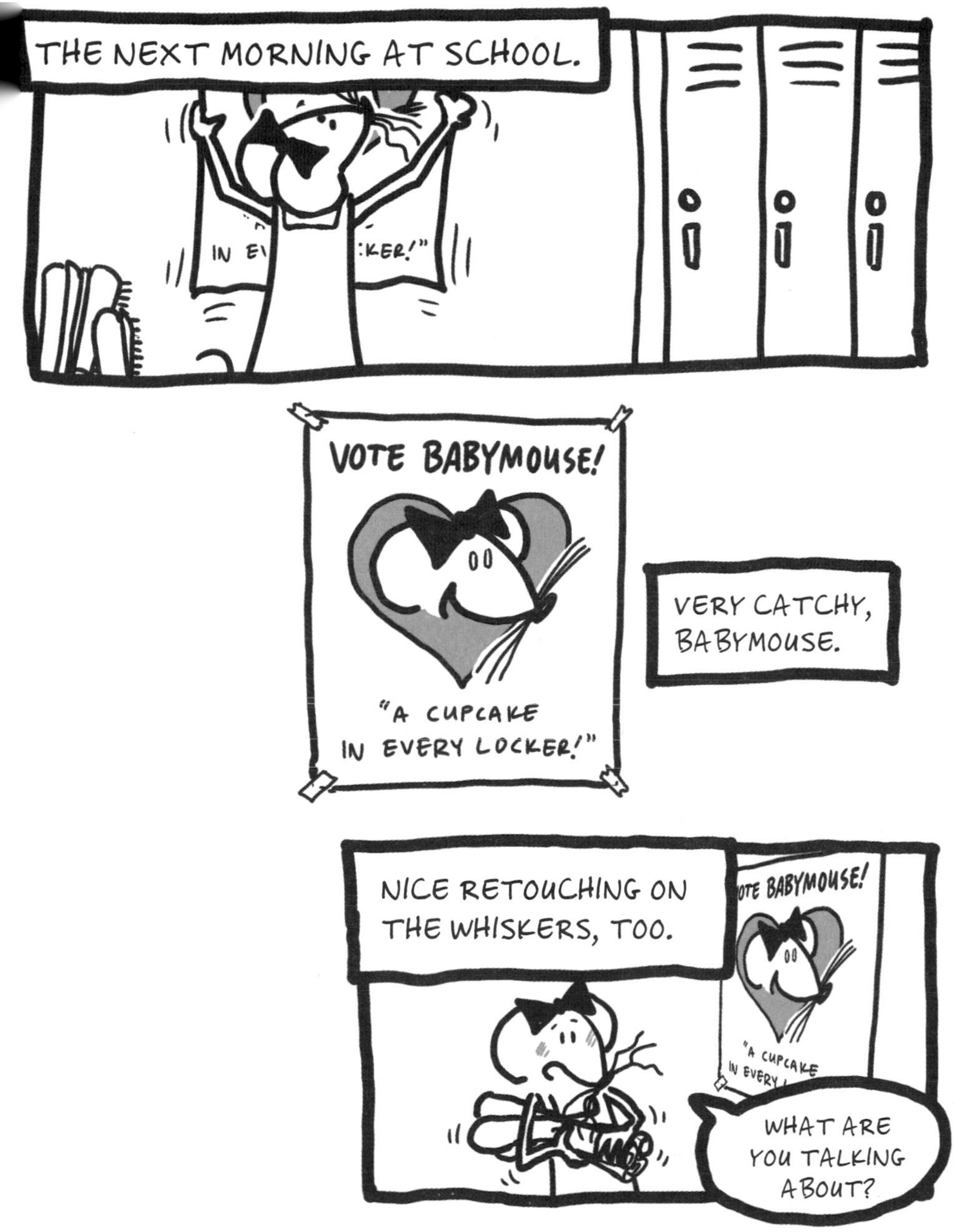
THE NEXT MORNING AT SCHOOL.
VOTE BABYMOUSE!
"A CUPCAKE IN EVERY LOCKER!"
VERY CATCHY, BABYMOUSE.
NICE RETOUCHING ON THE WHISKERS, TOO.
WHAT ARE YOU TALKING ABOUT?

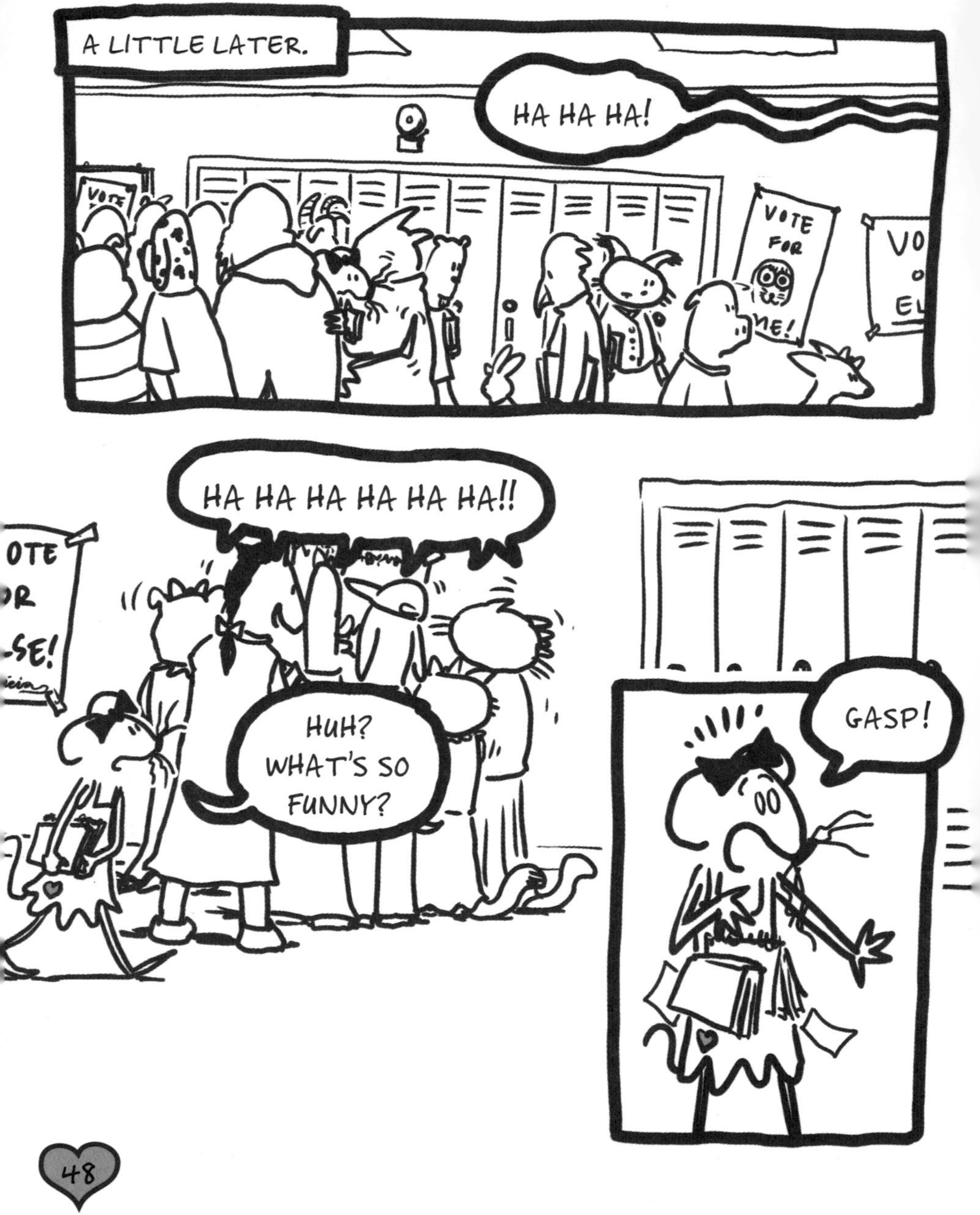
A LITTLE LATER.
HA HA HA!
VOTE FOR
HA HA HA HA HA HA!!
HUH? WHAT'S SO FUNNY?
GASP!

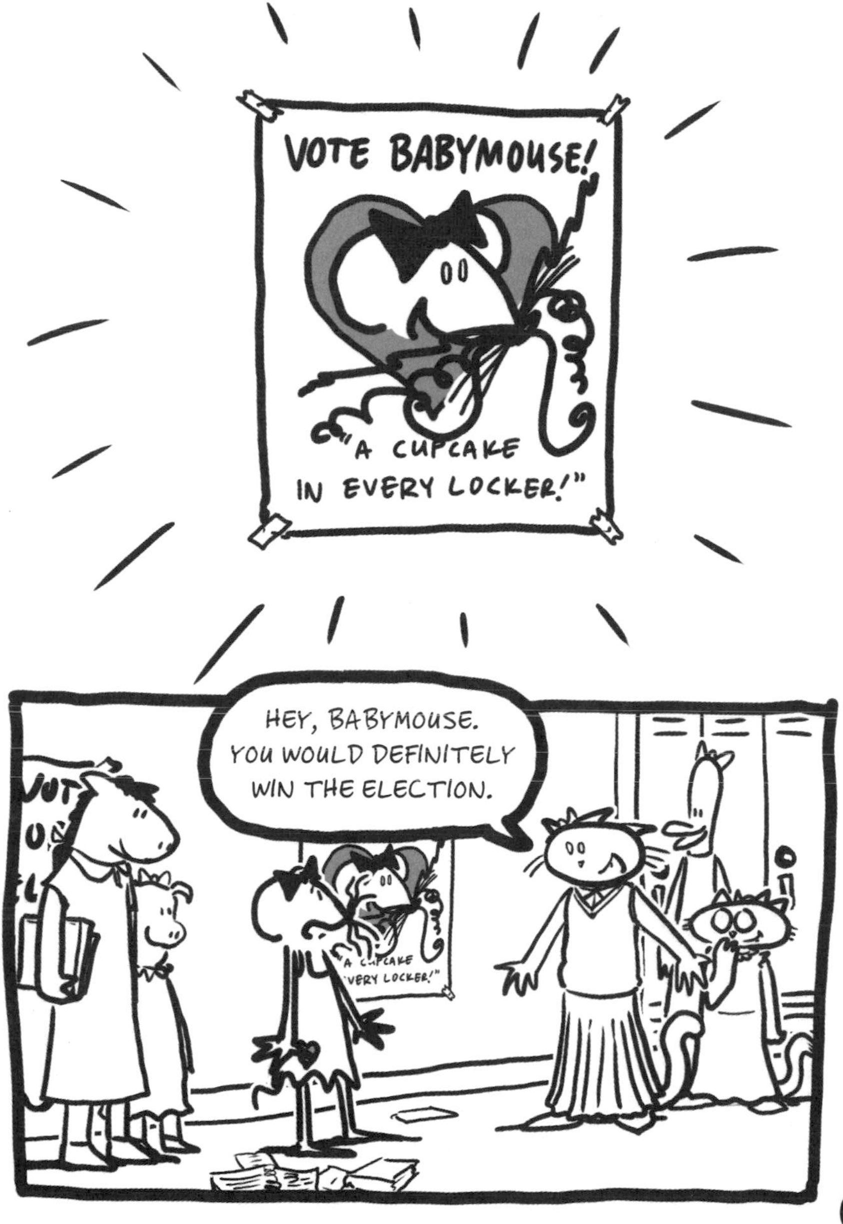
VOTE BABYMOUSE!
"A CUPCAKE IN EVERY LOCKER!"
HEY, BABYMOUSE. YOU WOULD DEFINITELY WIN THE ELECTION.

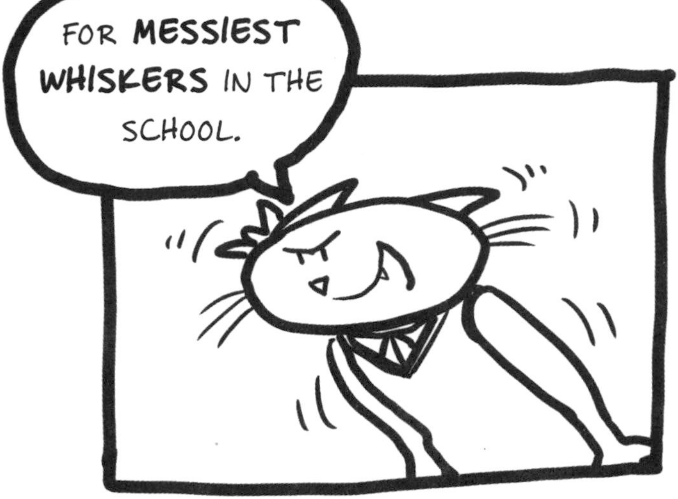
FOR **MESSIEST WHISKERS** IN THE SCHOOL.

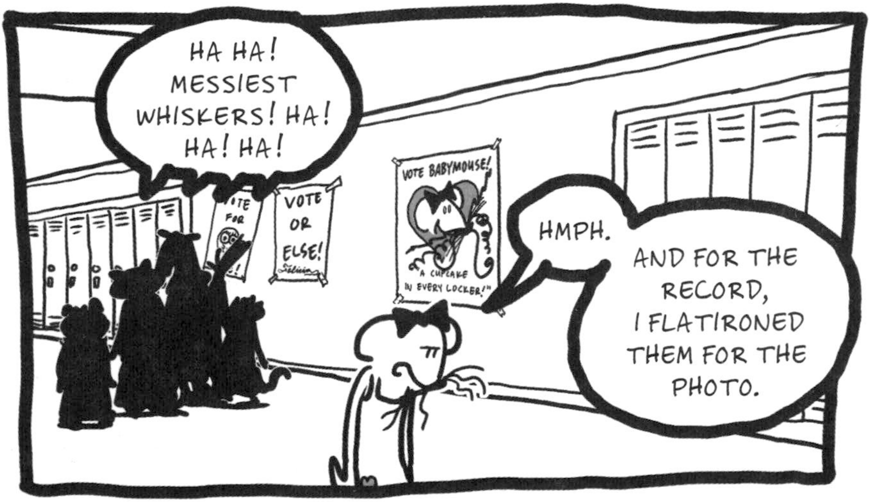
HA HA! MESSIEST WHISKERS! HA! HA! HA!
VOTE OR ELSE!
VOTE BABYMOUSE!
"A CUPCAKE IN EVERY LOCKER!"
HMPH.
AND FOR THE RECORD, I FLATIRONED THEM FOR THE PHOTO.

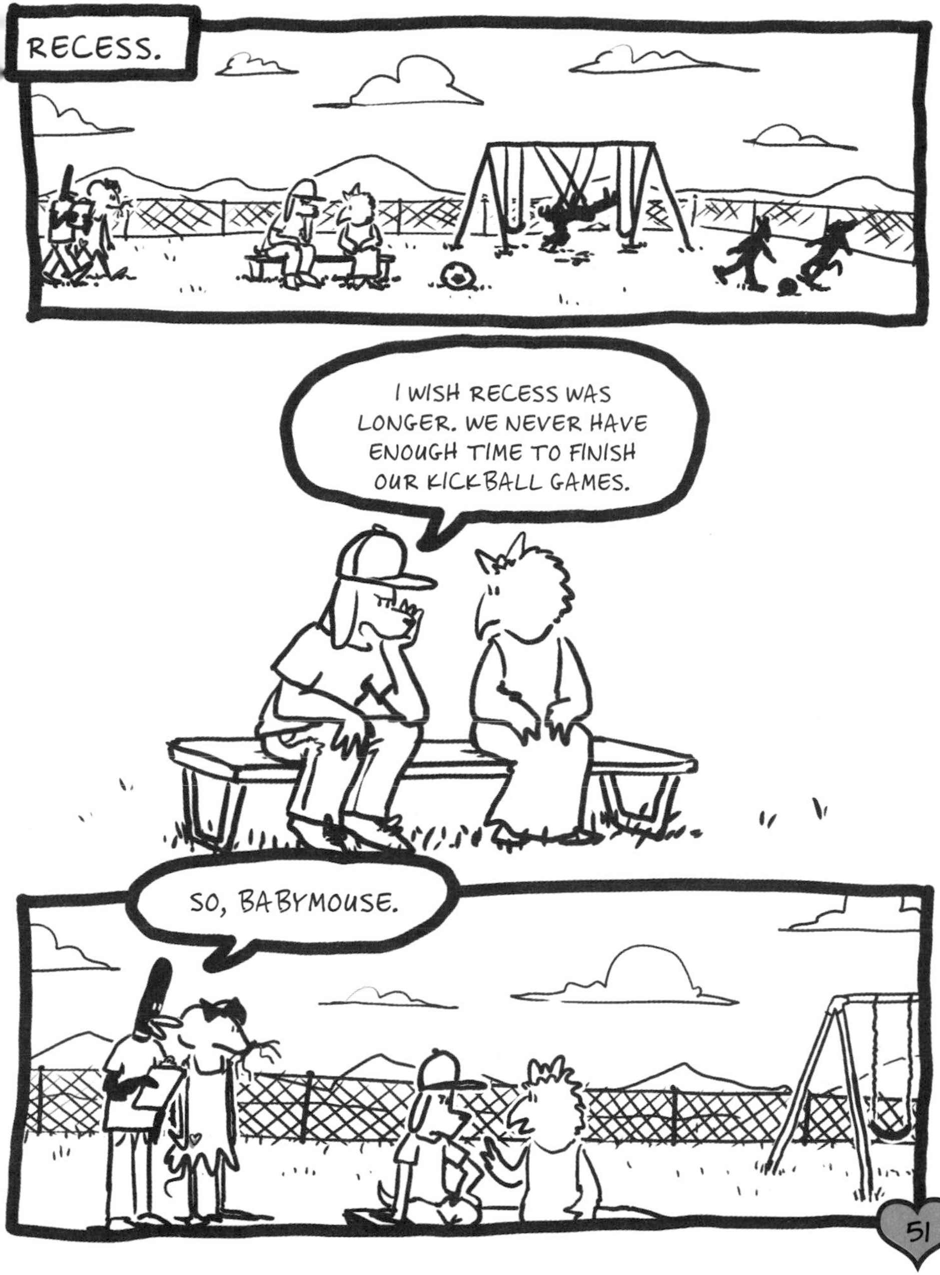
RECESS.
I WISH RECESS WAS LONGER. WE NEVER HAVE ENOUGH TIME TO FINISH OUR KICKBALL GAMES.
SO, BABYMOUSE.

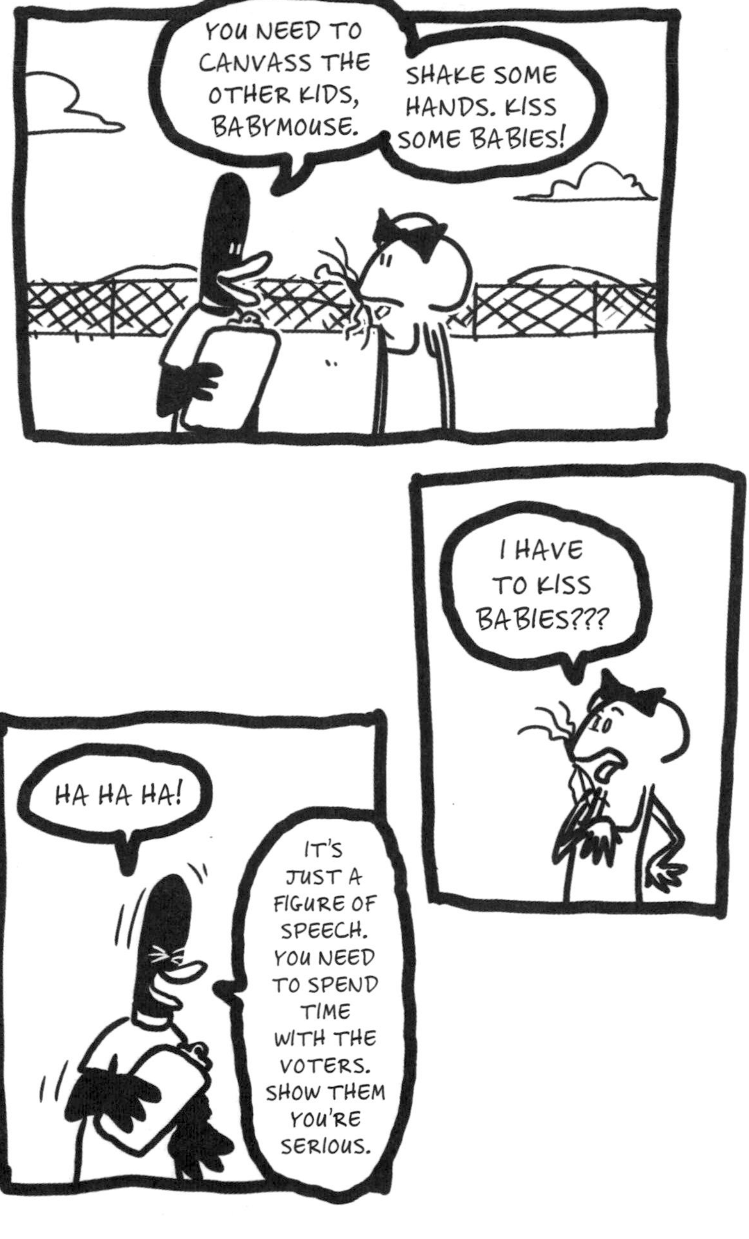
YOU NEED TO CANVASS THE OTHER KIDS, BABYMOUSE.
SHAKE SOME HANDS. KISS SOME BABIES!
I HAVE TO KISS BABIES???
HA HA HA!
IT'S JUST A FIGURE OF SPEECH. YOU NEED TO SPEND TIME WITH THE VOTERS. SHOW THEM YOU'RE SERIOUS.

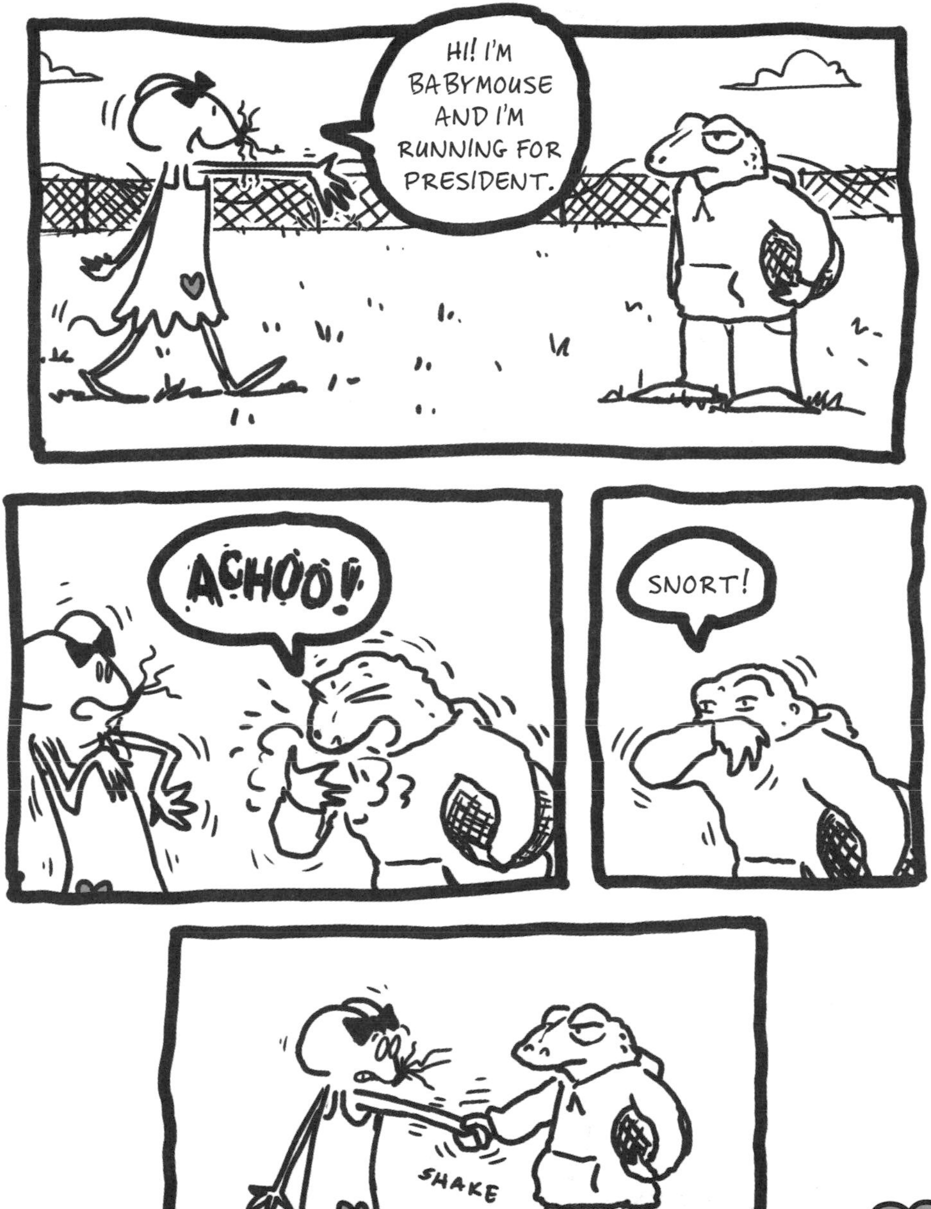
HI! I'M BABYMOUSE AND I'M RUNNING FOR PRESIDENT.
ACHOO!
SNORT!
SHAKE

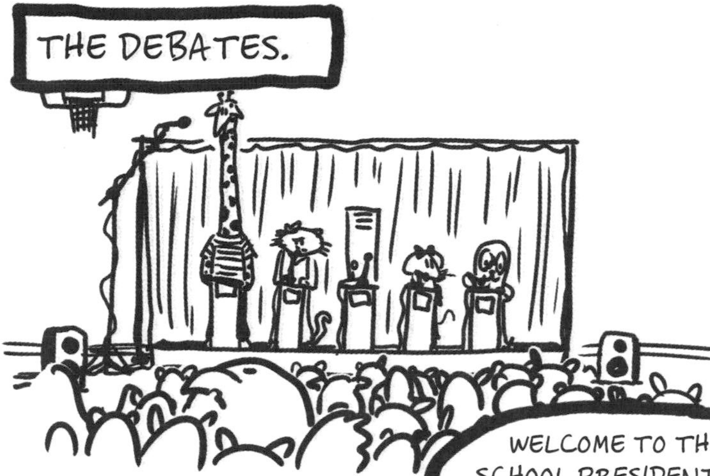
THE DEBATES.

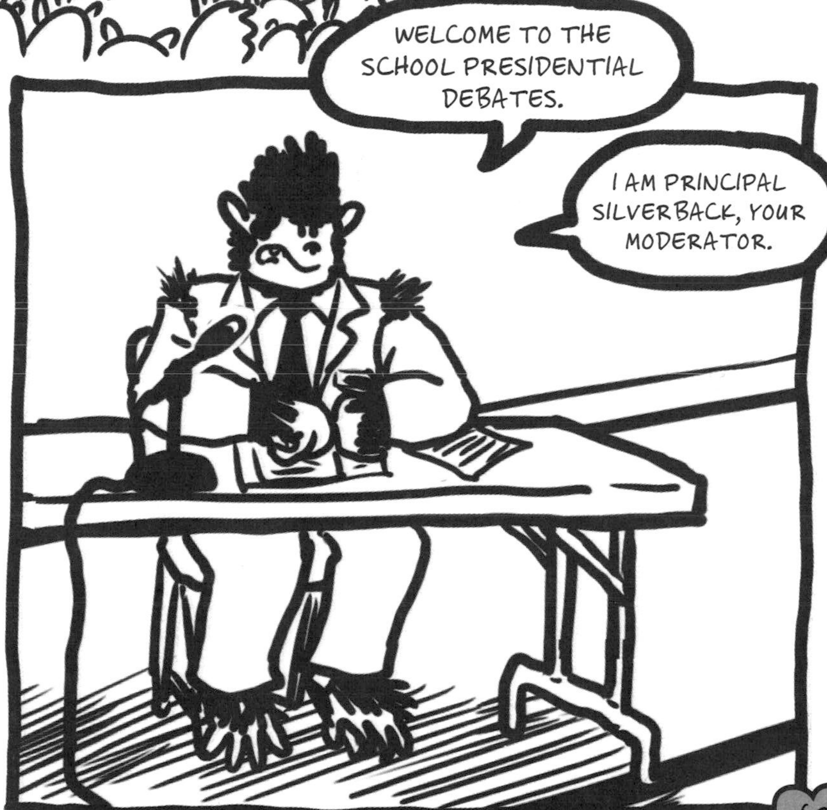
WELCOME TO THE SCHOOL PRESIDENTIAL DEBATES.
I AM PRINCIPAL SILVERBACK, YOUR MODERATOR.

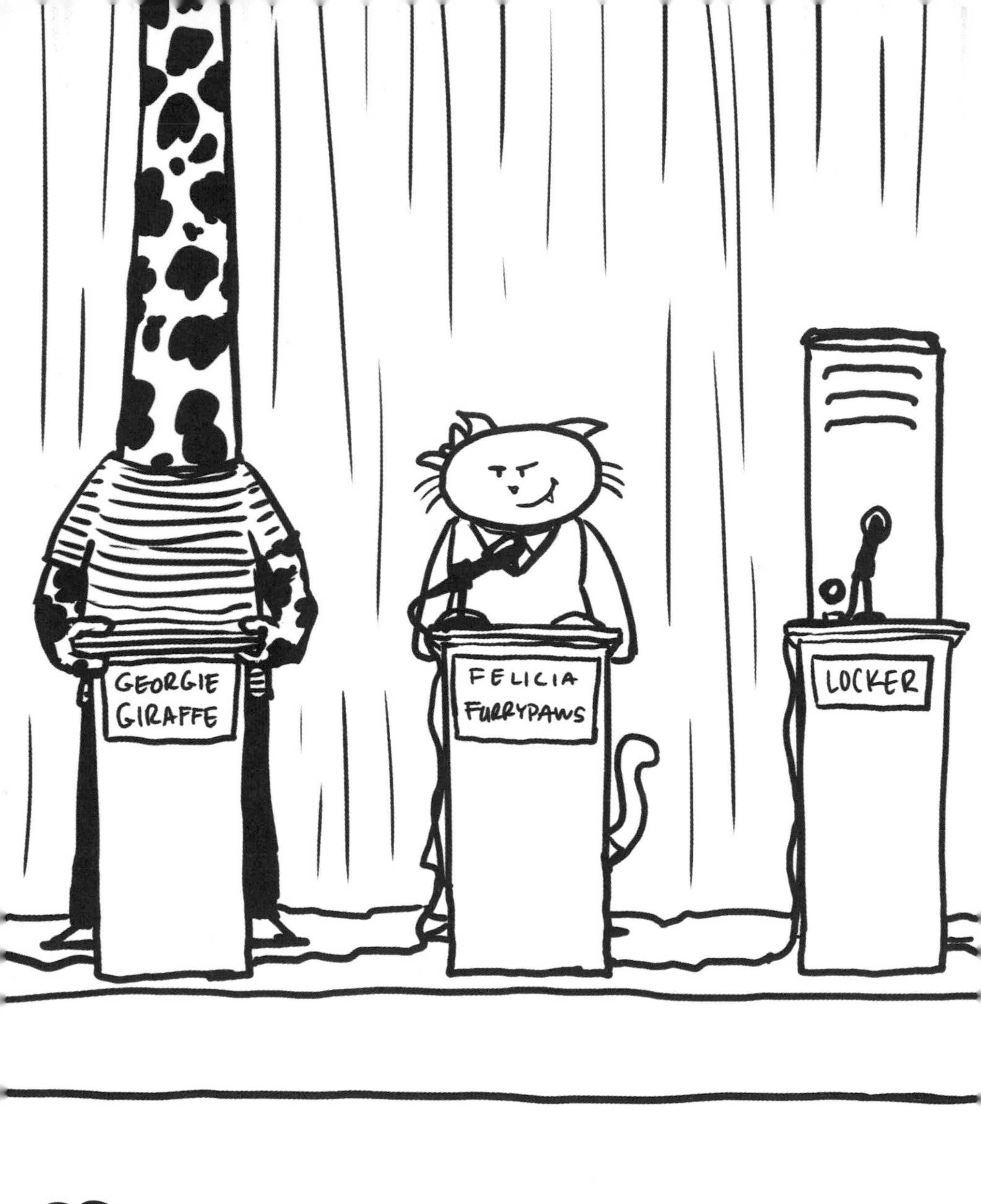
GEORGIE GIRAFFE
FELICIA FURRYPAWS
LOCKER

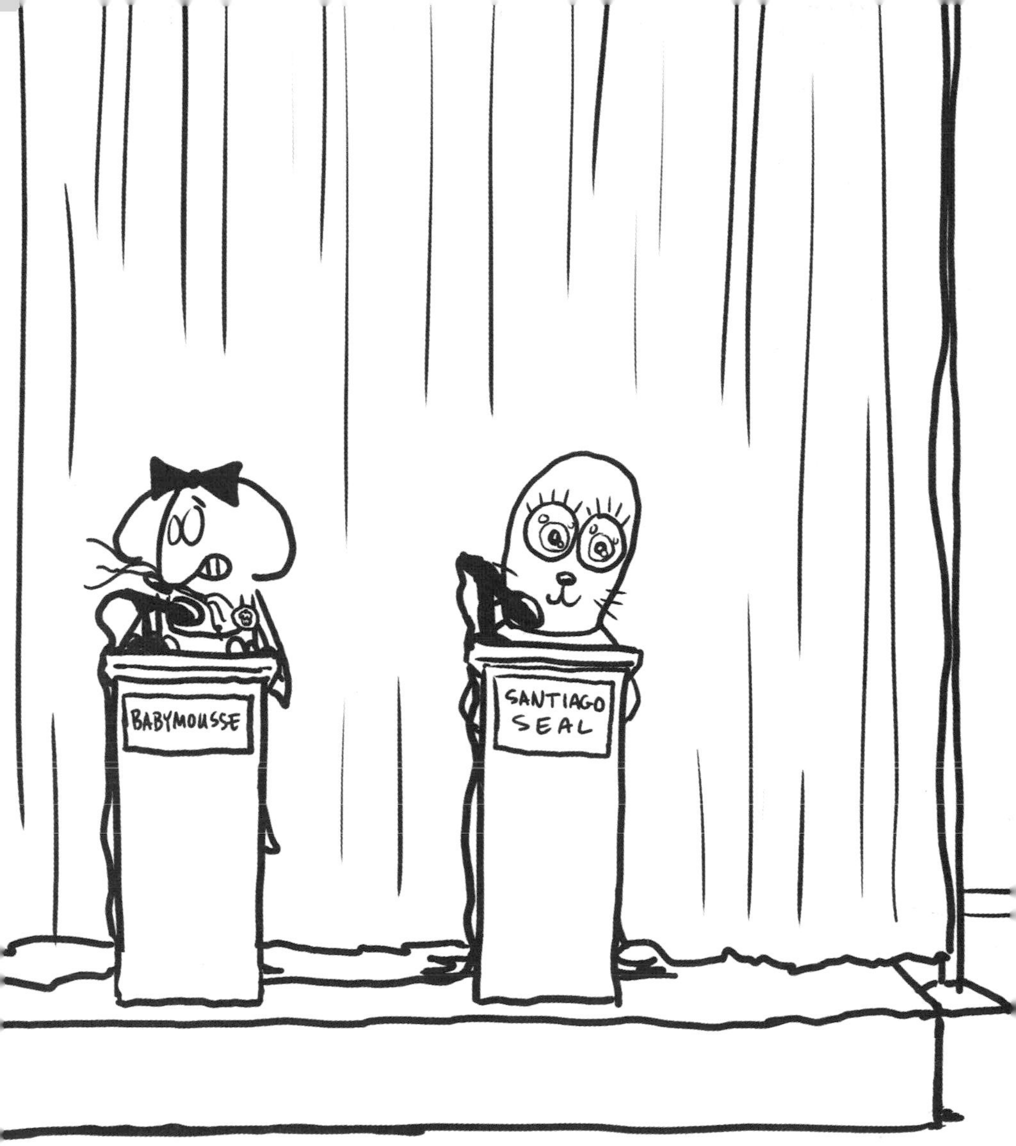
BABYMOUSSE
SANTIAGO
SEAL

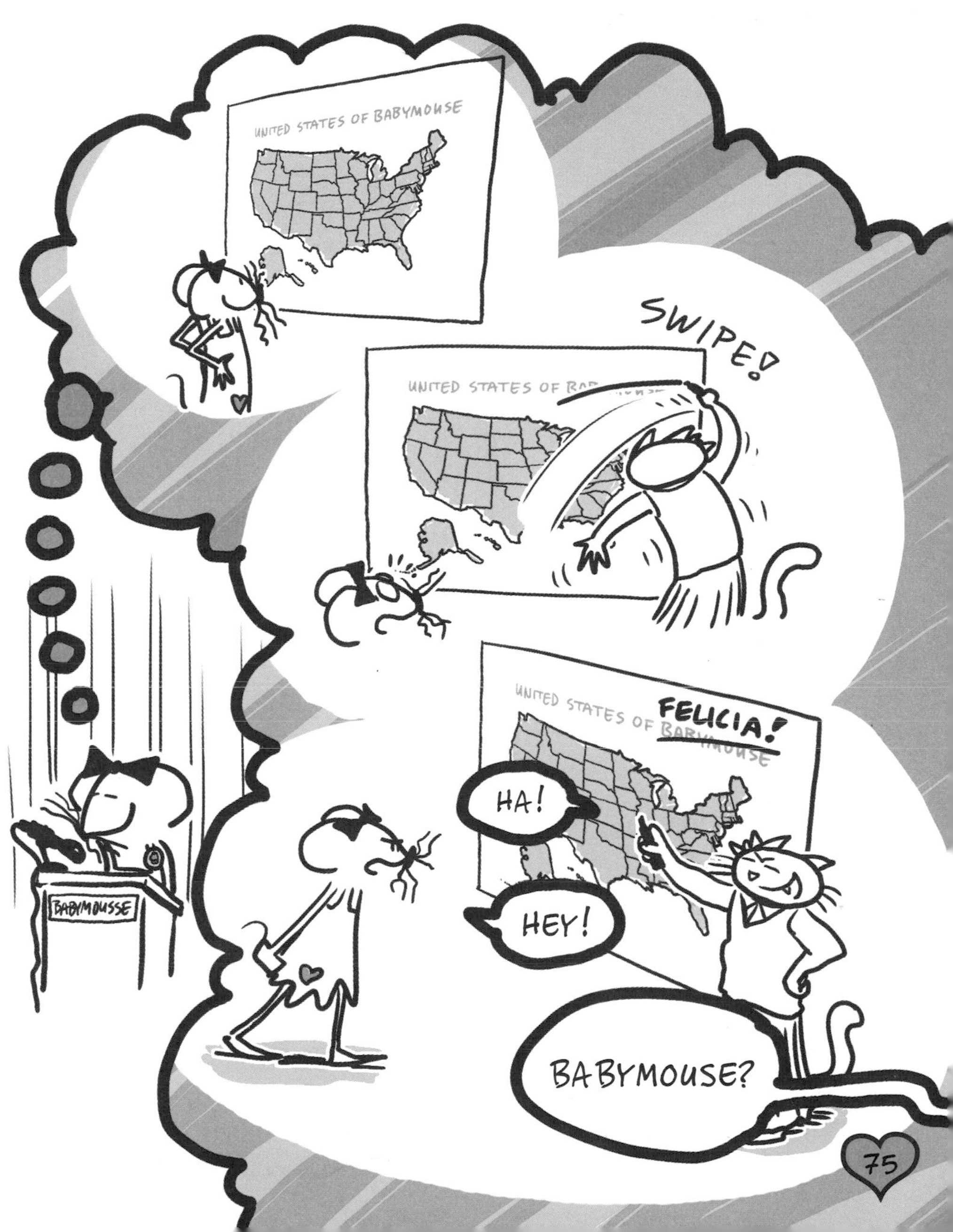

UNITED STATES OF BABYMOUSE
SWIPE!
UNITED STATES OF FELICIA!
HA!
HEY!
BABYMOUSSE
BABYMOUSE?

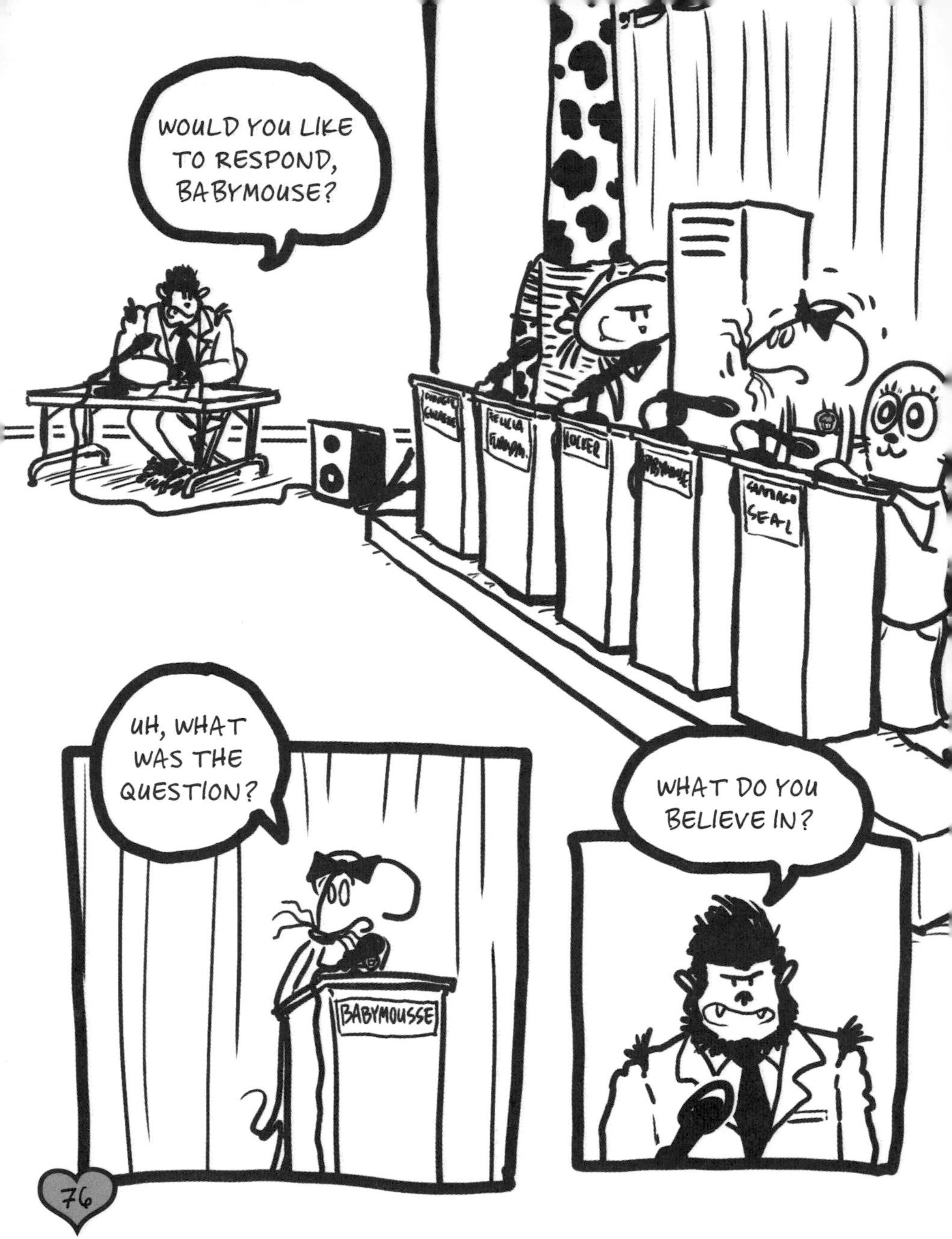
WOULD YOU LIKE TO RESPOND, BABYMOUSE?
UH, WHAT WAS THE QUESTION?
BABYMOUSSE
WHAT DO YOU BELIEVE IN?

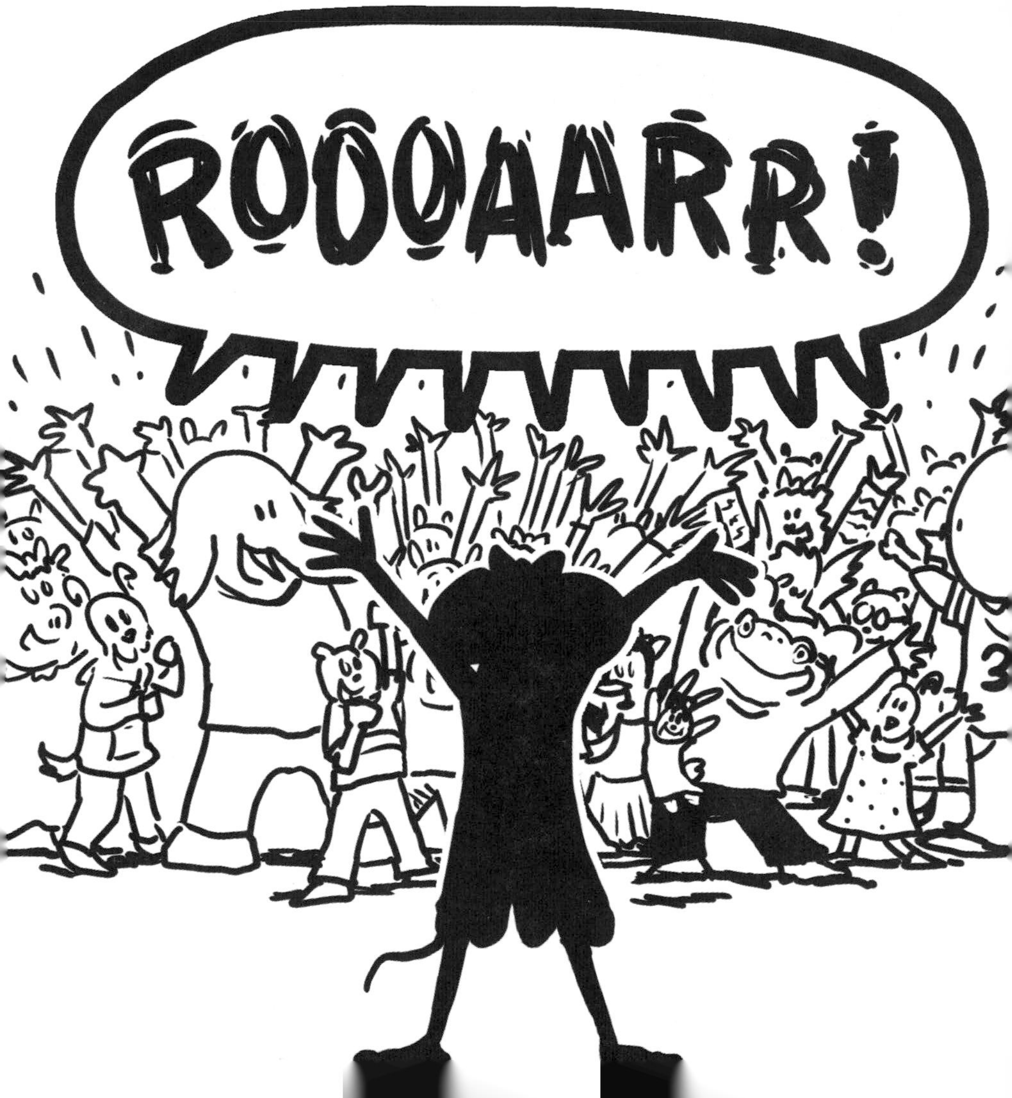
ROOOAARR!

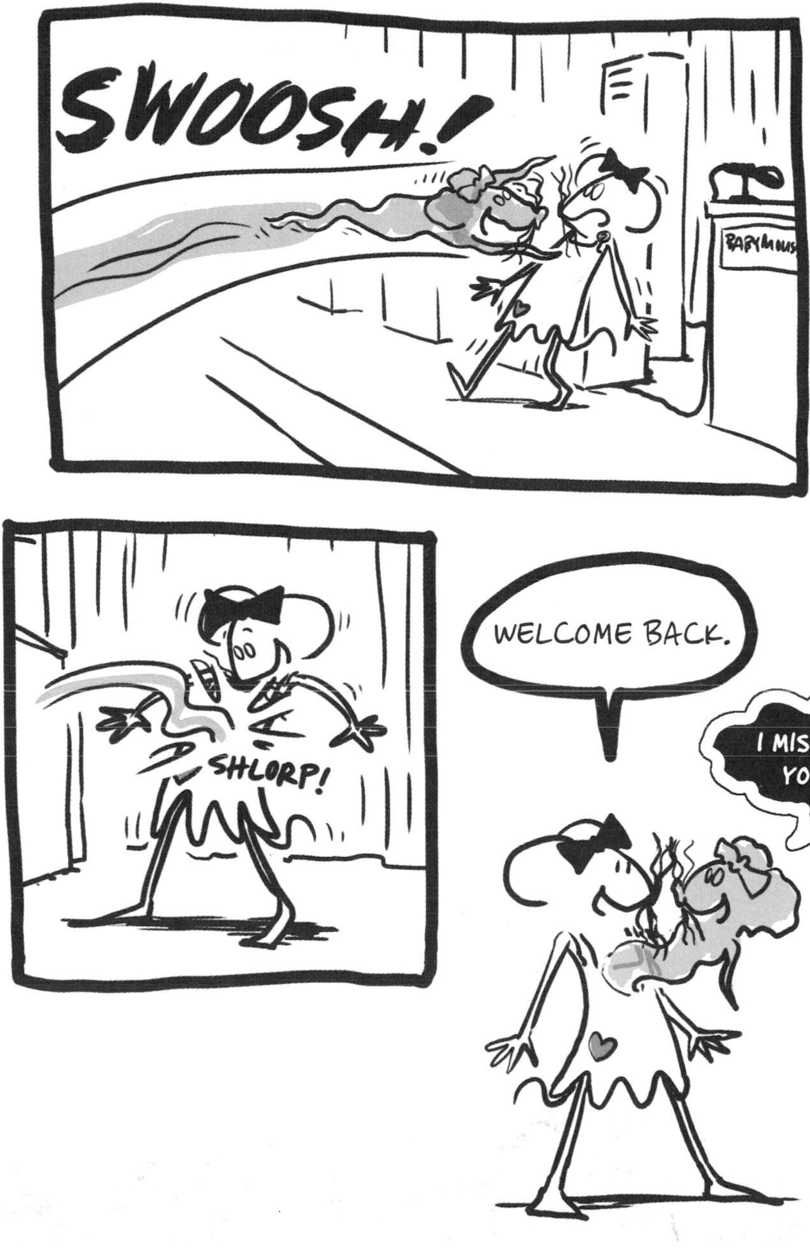
SWOOSH!
BABYMOUS
SHLORP!
WELCOME BACK.
I MISSED YOU.

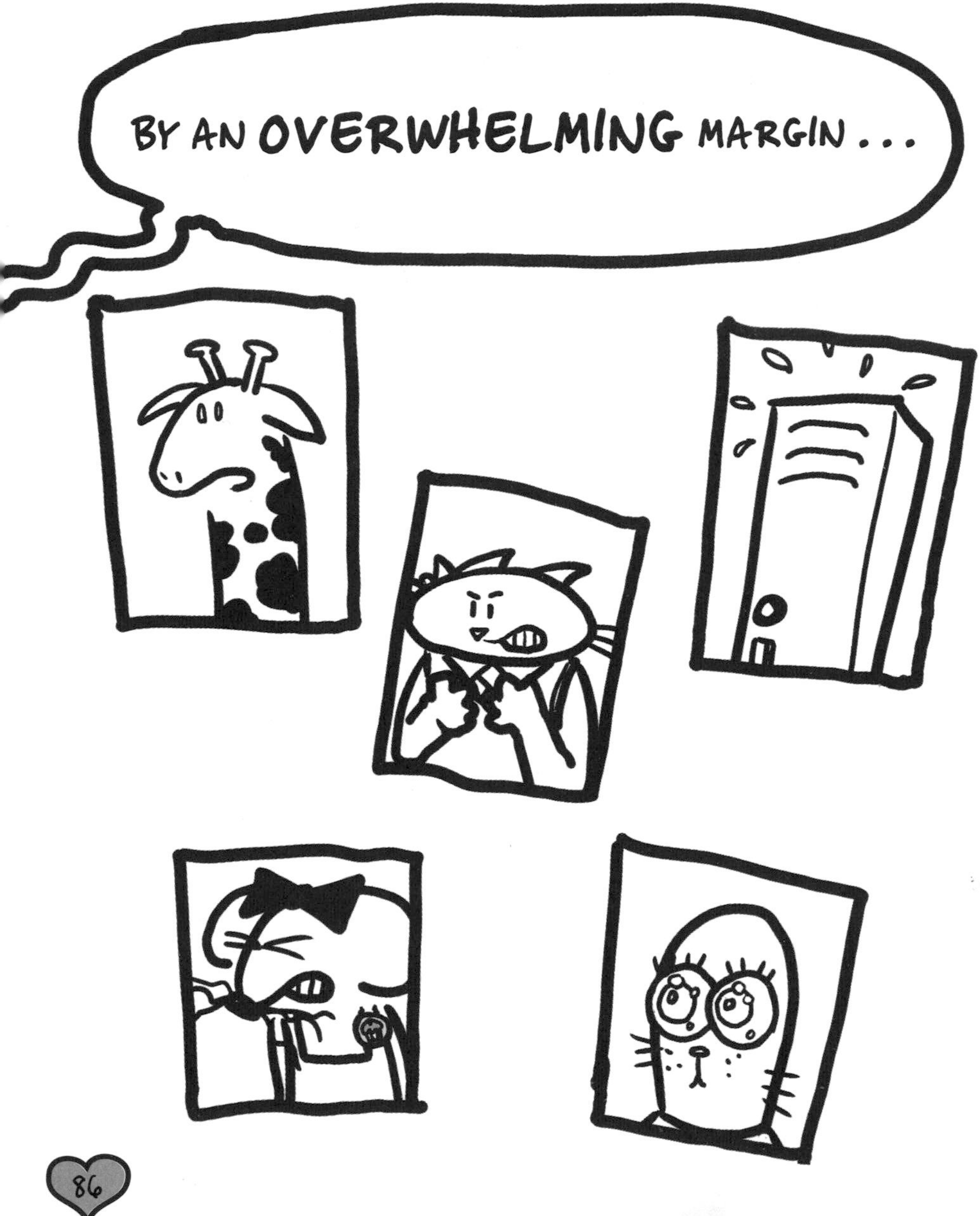
BY AN OVERWHELMING MARGIN . . .

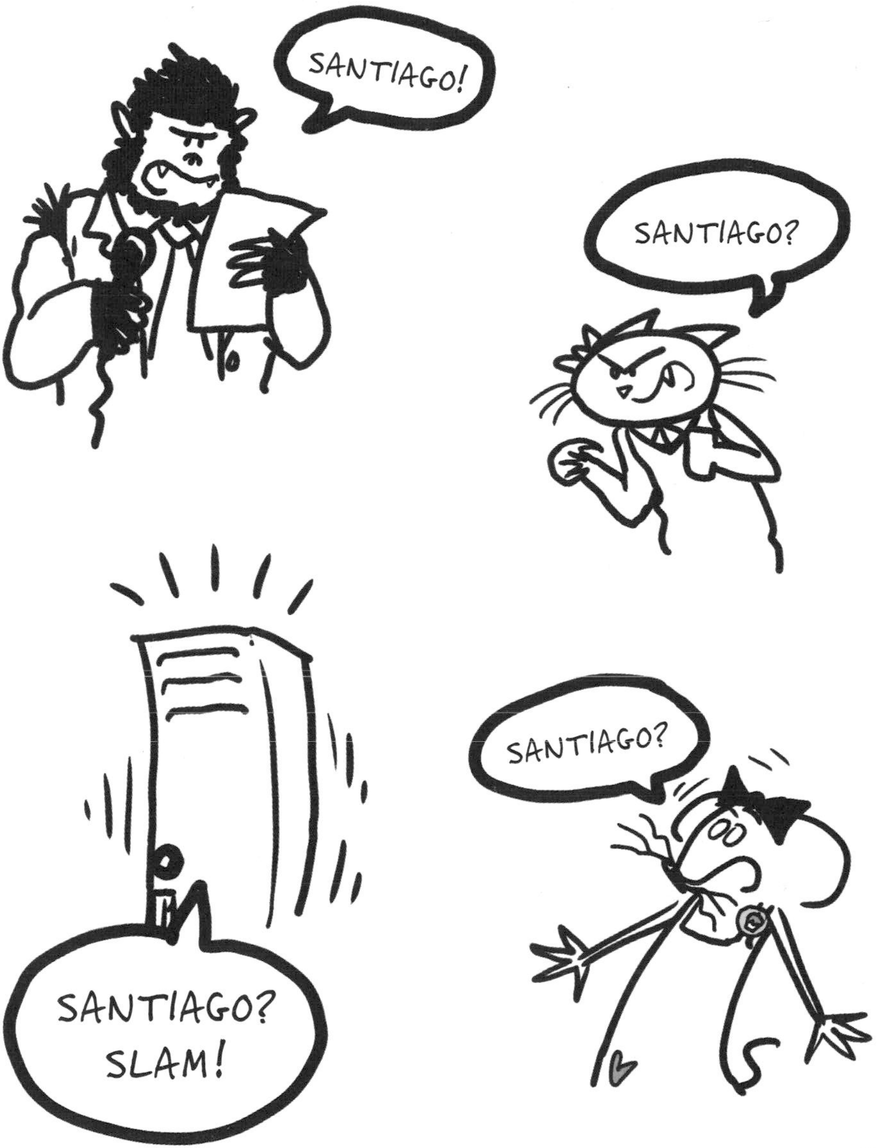
SANTIAGO!
SANTIAGO?
SANTIAGO?
SLAM!
SANTIAGO?

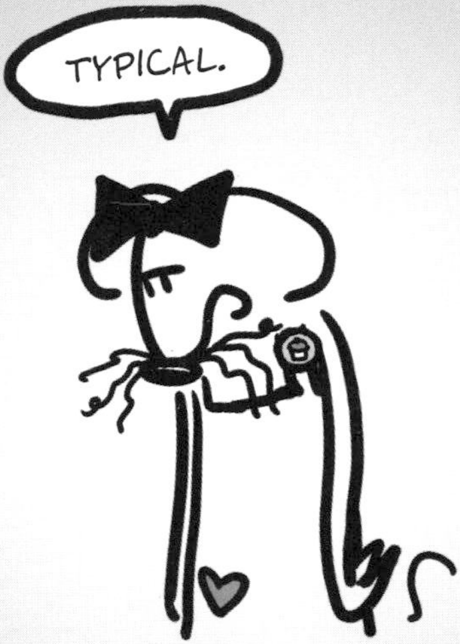
TYPICAL.

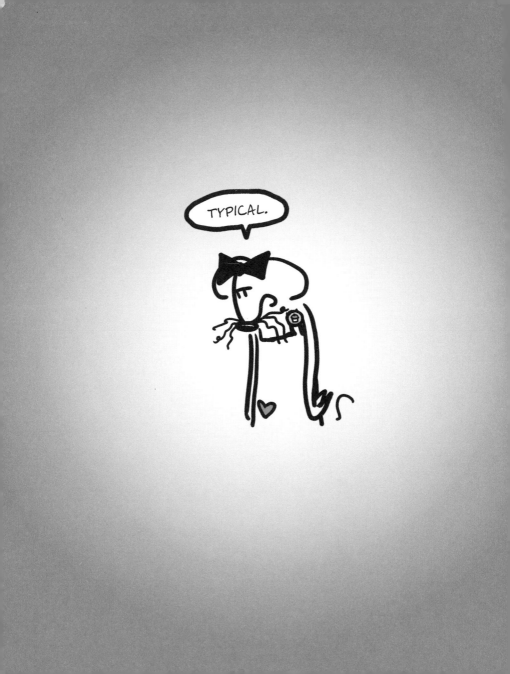

DON'T MISS THE NEXT BABYMOUSE!

EXTREME BABYMOUSE

COMING IN JANUARY 2013

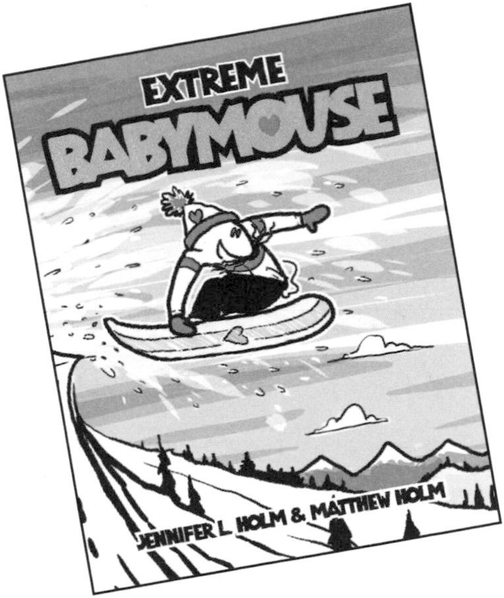
EXTREME
BABYMOUSE
JENNIFER L. HOLM & MATTHEW HOLM

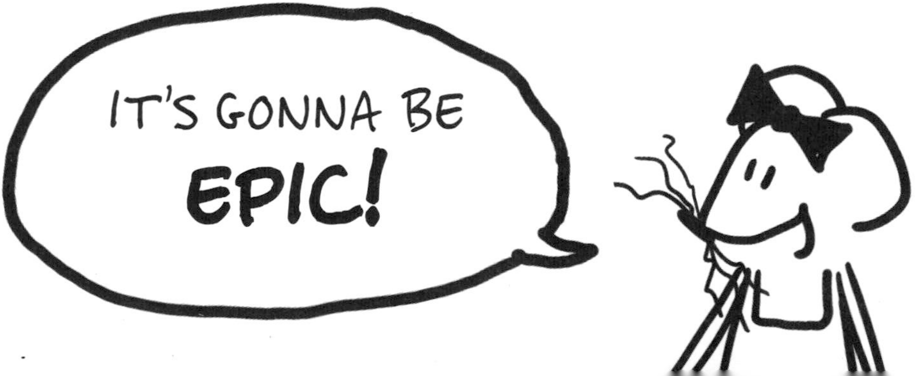
IT'S GONNA BE EPIC!

READ ABOUT
SQUISH'S AMAZING ADVENTURES IN:

★ "IF EVER A NEW SERIES DESERVED TO GO
VIRAL, THIS ONE DOES."
—KIRKUS REVIEWS, STARRED

you'll love these other great books
by Jennifer L. Holm!

THE BOSTON JANE TRILOGY
EIGHTH GRADE IS MAKING ME SICK
MIDDLE SCHOOL IS WORSE THAN MEATLOAF
OUR ONLY MAY AMELIA
PENNY FROM HEAVEN
TURTLE IN PARADISE

THEY'RE REALLY GOOD! TRUST ME!